FARCRY®

★ ★ ★ ★ ★

ABSOLUTION

A FAR CRY 5 NOVEL

FARCRY®

★ ★ ★ ★ ★

ABSOLUTION

URBAN WAITE

TITAN BOOKS

FAR CRY: ABSOLUTION

Print edition ISBN: 9781785659157
E-book edition ISBN: 9781785659164

Published by Titan Books
A division of Titan Publishing Group Ltd
144 Southwark Street, London SE1 0UP

First Titan edition: February 2018
10 9 8 7 6 5 4 3 2

This book is a work of fiction. Any references to historical events, real people, or real places are used fictitiously. Other names, characters, places, and events are products of the author's imagination, and any resemblance to actual events or places or persons, living or dead, is entirely coincidental.

Cover by Faceout Studio
Book design by dix!

Special thanks:
Yves Guillemot, Laurent Detoc, Alain Corre, Geoffroy Sardin, Yannis Mallat, Gérard Guillemot, Jean-Sébastien Décant, David Bédard, Manuel Fleurant, Dan Hay, Andrew Holmes, Nelly Kong, Marie-Joelle Paquin, Julia Pung, Sébastien Roy, Andrejs Verlisd, Sarah Buzby, Clémence Deleuze, Caroline Lamache, Victoria Linel, Anthony Marcantonio, François Tallec, Joshua Meyer, Virginie Gringarten, Marc Muraccini, Cécile Russeil, Raha Bouda, Stone Chin, Holly Hua, Jordan Archer, Bailey Mcandrews, Adam Climan, Heather Haefner, Barbara Radziwon, Damian Dale, Tom Curtis, Giancarlo Varanini, Lauren Jaques, Derek Thornton, Tina Cameron.

A CIP catalogue record for this title is available from the British Library.

Printed and bound by CPI Group (UK) Ltd, Croydon, CR0 4YY.

For the fans who make this real

PROLOGUE

The harvest is the end of the age, and the reapers are angels.

—MATTHEW 13:39

THE SHERIFF CAME IN AND SAT IN HIS CHAIR. HE TOOK OFF HIS hat, put up his feet, and looked across the desk at her. "What's this all about?" he said.

"You know what this is about," Mary May said. "I just want to know what you're going to do about it?"

The sheriff fingered the band of his hat, picked something off the brim and flicked it away. He had been a bull rider at one point and Mary May remembered him from when she had been a girl. Daddy and Mamma had brought her and her brother, Drew, to see this man ride. The man had been skinny then, and young. She had stood at the edge of the railing and watched him come out of the gates. They had hollered at him to stay on as he rode out into the center with the dirt kicking up under the bull and the man bouncing atop, barely able to hold on. He had seemed fearless in that moment. He had seemed like some sort of hero, but he did not seem like that now.

He tossed the hat on the table, took his feet down from the desk, and looked her straight in the eye. "Shit, Mary May, you know I can't do a thing about it. You know it wasn't nothing but an accident and even if it wasn't there's not a goddamn thing to be done."

"An accident? Daddy went out there to get Drew. Forty some years of driving trucks, his and anyone's he worked for, and he never even put a scratch on one of them. Now you're calling it an accident?"

"I'm sorry for your loss, but there's nothing that can be done."

She looked at him sitting there. She could see the genuine compassion in his eyes and she felt saddened for him because she knew that what he was saying was true. "You think they're ever going to push you too far? You think they're ever just going to push you so far you fall off the edge?"

"What are we talking about here?"

She smiled. She ran her eyes around the office and then back to the desk where his hat was sitting on the wood between them. She would turn thirty years old that fall. She had lost nearly all that she ever cared about and it seemed like it had happened overnight. The only thing she had left was the bar and the rage that had grown in her. "Drew is still out there," she said. "I plan on getting him back, or at least telling him our Daddy is dead. That's what I'm talking about." She pushed back from the desk and stood. She wore a T-shirt and jeans and her shoulder-length brown hair was tied up behind her head and she could feel the dangerous pulse of the blood tapping away in a vein in her neck, but she had no way of controlling it.

"I went out there once," he said, his voice stopping her in place, her hand on the metal doorknob of the office door. In the glass above, with the stenciled lettering across the window, she could see him standing now watching her.

"I was invited. They asked me if I'd come sit in on one of their services."

She turned.

He took a few steps and came around the desk. "We've got preppers, we've got doomsday freaks, we've got whole families of folks living in shacks up in the hills. No power. No water. Grandma and the great-grandkids sleeping three to a bunk while mommy and daddy make more. We've got gun nuts. We've got bunkers and compounds. We've got free thinkers, anarchists, nihilists, democrats, and god knows what else, but I'm telling you, what I saw up there at

Eden's Gate—the conviction they have, the goddamn power they gave to the words of The Father, it was infectious, it got damn near under my skin. And they're believers, you know? Every one of them. And that's not to say a bad thing about them, or to question their faith, but I tell you, it scared me more than anything I have yet seen in this life and there's not a thing I can do about that. Because, you know what, it's perfectly legal."

"You practice that?" Mary May asked.

"I tell it to myself every night before bed."

She turned to the door and opened it. "He's my brother. He's all I have left," she said, and walked out.

MARY MAY WAS HALFWAY UP THE MOUNTAIN WHEN SHE SAW THE white church truck appear in her rearview. It followed her for another five miles. She raised her eyes on it at every turn of the road, watching the far trees and the bend of the asphalt where the road disappeared, but the truck never wavered. Always appearing again from out of the curve and following along as if the two—her red Ford pickup and the white church pickup—had been tethered together with rope, one dragging the other right behind.

She went another mile before she pulled over on the side of the road and turned off the engine. She brought up her father's old chrome-plated .38 and set it on the dash before her. If there was someone to call she would have done it right then, but there was no one to call and no signal to get in all of Hope County so she waited for the white truck to break from around the last curve.

When the truck pulled into the gravel behind her, she recognized the man sitting in the driver's seat. John Seed. She had known him for almost half her life and she had, at one time, thought of him as just another human being in this world, but not anymore. He was something dangerous to her and to any that seemed to chance across his way. He and his brothers ran Eden's Gate and if anyone knew what had happened to her father, or where she might be able to find her brother, it was John Seed.

She watched him push open the door and then stand. He was ten years older than her and near six foot with brown hair and a beard that covered the lower half of his face. In the mirror, she could see how he kept his eyes on her then reached back inside the truck and brought something out of the cab. Mary May thought maybe it was a gun but she could not be sure. He lifted the tail of his shirt and hid away whatever it was. When he walked up to her she had already cracked her window.

"You scared?" John asked.

She looked at him. "Should I be?"

He stood there a few seconds more and then he put a hand out and ran his fingers across the top of her window, his fingertips within the cab. "You got a license for that thing?" he asked, nodding to the gun on the dash, his fingertips lingering on the top of the window before he took them back.

Her eyes went to the gun and then she looked back on John where he'd taken a step back and stood a little way apart from her truck, like maybe he expected her to use it. "It was Daddy's," she said.

She watched him. He seemed to be considering what the right response might be. "I was sorry to hear about him," John said, and she thought, well, that almost sounded human.

"He was coming up here to get Drew when it happened."

"Is that right?"

"Now I'm coming up to get Drew and tell him to come home."

"I heard about that, too."

"You have?"

"Sure," John said. "I hear all kinds of things from the people I know. I hear you all are still serving alcohol even though we asked you not to. That's just one of the things I hear."

She looked at him as if he might be stupid, but she knew very well that he was not. "How do you expect me to keep running a bar with no alcohol?"

"I don't."

He said it very matter-of-fact and she knew he meant it. "You know where my brother is?"

"I know where he is. He's with us."

"Does he know about Daddy?"

"He knows."

"You going to let him come down off the mountain?"

"He can come down off the mountain any time it pleases him. I'm not his keeper."

"That right?"

"That's what I'm saying to you."

She put her hand to the key and cranked the ignition then sat there with her hands on the steering wheel. The chrome-plated .38 was still on the dash and it vibrated in time with the engine.

"Where are you going?"

"I'm going to get my brother."

"Look," he said. "You're a smart girl."

She hated him for saying it like that, as if he knew something better than she did.

He came forward a bit and she raised a hand up the wheel and her eyes went to the gun again.

"All this isn't necessary," he said. "Why don't you turn around and go back down the mountain before something happens that can't be undone?"

Instead of answering, she put the truck in drive and left him standing there. In the rearview she saw him take the thing he had placed beneath the tail of his shirt and raise it to his lips. It was a radio and she knew whatever he was using it for probably concerned her, and was probably also not good.

After a mile, she took down the .38 and placed it beneath her thigh, keeping pressure on it so that it would not slide away as she continued up the mountain, taking each curve in the road and looking up at the rearview each time, half expecting to see John still following her.

When she came around the next curve of the road she saw two church trucks waiting crossways. Four men stood there, each of them carrying what she could only guess from this distance was a rifle or even a machine gun. She stopped the truck and took the gun from beneath her thigh and flipped open the cylinder to look in on the casings. She had half a mind just to turn around. But she knew that she wouldn't, to give up now was to give up on her brother and all that he'd ever meant to her, all that had been her family and that her father had fought so fiercely to preserve.

She pushed the transmission into reverse and threw a hand up across the bench seat and then slammed down on the gas pedal. The truck tires spun and she was moving now, going backwards on the road, thinking of a small gravel logging road she'd seen that went up the mountain. When she came around the curve just before the gravel road she saw John coming up along the mountain in his own truck.

For only a moment she thought of her father. She thought of how they had found him, bent over the wheel, the front windshield cracked and the big truck buckled and bent. There had been no witnesses, no evident cause for what had happened to him, but he was dead now and he had gone out just like she was, trying to bring back her brother. She thought of John's words, what had been said, what he had meant and she knew almost beyond a doubt that her father had not died in an accident.

Mary May did not slow as she came up on John, instead she mashed down on the gas and with the engine whining she cut the wheel hard to the left as soon as she saw the gravel offshoot and then bounced off the road. She was going backwards now up the mountain, the gravel catching in the tires and pinging in the wheel wells and when she turned to glance back through the front windshield she could see John following through the dust of her tires.

Down on the roadway the two other church trucks had turned in, one after the other, and followed John up the logging road.

Mary May took this all in as she drove, the engine blaring and the speedometer reading forty miles an hour as she kept going in reverse. There was nowhere on the narrow road to turn around so she kept her foot to the pedal, her arm up over the bench, her eyes on the road. The gravel had disappeared, she was driving on sodden dirt lined on all sides by the thick growth of alpine forest. The truck splashing through puddles with the mud tossed into the air by the tires and landing against the rear window. The rear bed of her truck seen as it bounced up out of a deep puddle looking like the hull of some boat breaking through muddy brown waves. The window gradually clouding with the spray off the tires.

When she hit whatever it was that she hit—a rock or a branch laid out in the road—she was still going forty miles per hour. It was enough to send the truck sliding sideways on the road. She tried to brake and spin the wheel, something caught . . . the truck went airborne, crashing over the side of the road into the forest beyond.

I

Those who put their hands upon our ark, those who mean to drown us in the flood, those who want to cast us aside after all our toil—they will find any hand they put upon us will be severed and taken from their arm. Cut from them just as easily as the farmer, after all his labor, now bends to reap his wheat.

—THE FATHER, EDEN'S GATE
Hope County, Montana

THE BEAR WAS A BIG BOAR GRIZZLY DOWN OUT OF CANADA. Thunder had woken Will Boyd and he had come out into the night and looked to the north where the silhouette of the Northern Rockies stood like dark sentries amid the lighter gray of cloud and moon. The storm was somewhere to the north. He had felt it building all through the day as he worked, the air growing thick and that damp heavy feel that built with it. Erased in a second as the rain came down and the sky lit and cracked open like shattered lake ice soon subsumed by the pool of water it had grown from.

Six or seven miles away on the slope of the mountain he could see how the rain had started to fall in sheets, pushed forward on the wind. He stood and watched it from his place on the hill. The forest all around him, lodgepole pine and white spruce, and farther down in the hummock between foothills and forests he could see how the lightning lit and expanded across the field of Junegrass below.

He had crossed that same field many times in the past twelve years or so. He knew what it looked like in full spring bloom, filled with purple harebell and blue flax. In the summer, much of it gone to golden green and then brown all through the fall, until it sat scraped to a flat land of white for six months of the year. He crossed this field in bitter cold and deep fetid summer, moving down from the cabin he'd been given, across land the church had charged him with watching over, carrying with him the two plastic buckets he used to collect his water. Often, he would see elk or deer, sometimes a hawk or eagle circling high above.

Now he stood above this field, wrapped in the same wool blanket he had taken from his bed and he watched the far rain being pushed from ridge to ridge as if the wind were a thing to be seen and touched. The first rumble of thunder had woken him from his sleep and he had walked out into the blue night and waited, watching the far mountain. The lightning crashed a second time and the thunder followed a few moments later. The surrounding hills and mountains lit anew in that electric light of blue and white. Will pulled the blanket closer around his shoulders, moving forward a little, watching the pulse of light fade away and letting his eyes adjust again. The lightning had forked and branched and when he closed his eyes he could still see it there captured in the blackness beneath his lids.

What he saw first was the deer, a full-grown buck, just beginning to grow its antlers for the year. When the lightning struck again it had come halfway across the field in the darkness. Caught moving, frozen in time by the bolt of lightning from above, one of its front legs outstretched and the two powerful back legs caught mid-bound as the animal appeared to float across the field. Will saw this animal and then saw it disappear again, the lightning fading from the sky and the boom of the thunder soon following, the storm now grown closer and the foothills far out beginning to disappear within the rain.

He took several steps farther into the grass and sedge in search of the buck, but in the spare seconds it had shown itself it was gone again, rushed across the field as if in flight.

The big grizzly then came into the field. A shape of humped muscle moving in that greater darkness just before the storm, all upper body and lean moving muscle beneath that coat of fur. Ears pushed back along its head as it moved in great haste and speed. The lightning sparking high above and the bear pictured there like something seen standing within the depths of some great museum hall—large and fierce.

But when the lightning faded away, followed by the boom, the bear was still there, drawn up short, halfway across the field. The first few droplets of rain were coming now, pushed forward on the wind ahead of the storm. The bear seemed to test the air, raising its snout toward the far trees and the coming sheet of rain. When it stood on its two back legs and turned to face the rain, Will could not believe the size of the animal. He saw in it some primordial being that was half man and half beast, which might in days of yesteryear have ruled them all.

The bear stayed just that way, standing on hind legs to face the rain, as the sheet of water broke from the trees and moved in a wall across the field. The water enveloping all it passed across, so thick with droplets that everything behind—mountain, foothill, forest— had all but disappeared. When the rain hit the bear, it was like the bear had never been there at all and Will stood for a second longer, watching as the sheet of water climbed the hill toward him and soon was all around. Wind and water, crashing branches twenty or thirty feet above—no field or forest to be seen and Will turning now, as the water began to soak the blanket, and he went back toward his small cabin, opened the door, and threw himself within.

After an hour of listening to the rain pelt the thin tin of his roof above and the wind rattle the glass within the wood casements of his windows, Will opened the door and stood looking out at the night from within the frame. The moon had appeared again and small silver droplets of rainwater could be seen in places where they hung and then fell from blades of grass and the needles of the pines. Far overhead the blinking navigation lights of a jetliner crossed in the starry darkness like some visitor from another world.

It would take him three days before he caught sign of the bear again.

THE FIRST SIGN HE FOUND OF THE BIG GRIZZLY WAS A PRINT IN the loose mud of a stream a mile east of his place. Will stood looking down at it for a long while before he brought his eyes up and considered the dense growth of underbrush that lined the far side of the stream. Lush and green and nearly impenetrable.

He had come down toward the stream on a game trail and until this point he had seen no sign of the bear in the surrounding country. Mostly he tracked game and ran a series of trap lines for the church, his time divided between church and remote wilderness. Three weeks of every month spent tracking and hunting, then one week spent at Eden's Gate. In the three days that had passed since he'd seen the bear he had thought he would chance across some sign—find a tuft of hair, scat, or claw mark in the earth or up high on one of the pine trunks—but he never did.

At sixty-two, Will could not remember seeing a bear of this size ever in his life, and he wondered now what had drawn the big boar down out of the north into this valley. Many of the animals had moved on years before, hunted or chased away as the valley succumbed to farming and herding. Will needed to go farther and farther afield to catch his own game—deer and elk, turkey, beaver, and rabbit.

Wearing the old wide-brimmed hat, stained with his own salt, he was square-jawed beneath his beard. The muscles beneath his shirt still strong from hauling his ass up one hill and down the other on a daily basis. Now, he scanned the surroundings, his eyes roaming over the forest behind and then the underbrush across the stream. Will looked again to the print in the mud. He knelt, feeling the weight of his pack fall across his back as he spread his fingers and placed them atop the print. With his other hand, he held tight to the rifle strap, not wanting the old Remington to swing from his shoulder.

The shape of the print was larger than his spread hand by at least an inch on all sides. Will guessed he was likely looking at the front right paw. The long claw marks visible atop each toe, where they had further punctured the mud a couple inches farther on.

He rose and followed the stream in the direction the paw mark had suggested. When he came to the beaver dam about a quarter mile upstream he knelt out of sight and watched the fat little mammals swimming in the pond beyond.

Not quite in the center of the pond was the lodge they had built for themselves. He watched as one of the beavers emerged from the water and then, using teeth and squat front arms, began to fit a branch over what looked to be a fresh hole dug into the side of the lodge. Many of the old logs showing the telltale claw marks of the bear where it had dug into the meat of the wood.

He saw no more sign of the bear as he went on, following the little stream that flowed down out of the mountains and made its way through the foothills. He set rabbit snares and then circled back around to a separate string he had placed the day before and found three out of six held white-tailed jackrabbits.

He broke their necks quickly with a practiced efficiency that had come from years of experience. Skills and knowledge his own father and grandfather before him had handed down to him. When he had checked and reset all six of the snares he carried the rabbits off to the stream and then gutted them, running the carcasses through the cool water at a place he favored, where bare rock ran flat and wide into the stream.

Many times Will had bathed here, washing his clothes in the stream and then leaving them to dry in the sun while he swam naked in the long, deep pool beyond. His hands and face tanned dark and brown from the spring and summer and the rest of his body—except for a patch of scar tissue across his chest where a tattoo had once been—was white and almost luminescent in the clear glacial melt.

Now he knelt at the water's edge. He worked the innards from the rabbits until the carcasses were clean. The last trail of blood wafted like smoke in the slow-moving pool, the current pulling the blood along before blending this last strand of red into the greater flow.

When he looked up again the bear was watching him from out of the opposite edge of the forest. Will saw the hump of muscle across the shoulder and the broad powerful forelegs gripping the edge of the bank as it watched him, its dull black eyes and the scooped front barrel of its face turned on him. The nose wet, bits of dirt and grass visible in places from whatever the bear had been scavenging nearby. Will did not move. His rifle, a twenty-year-old bolt-action Remington 700, lay five feet up the rock with his pack and what remained of his snares. He stayed crouched over the water with the rabbit carcasses beside him on the rock, his hunting knife in one hand.

He watched the bear test the air once before it turned, moving down the opposite side of the stream to where the pool ran out into shallow water. Will was up now, holding the rabbits and knife, backing toward the pack and rifle. The bear turned and rose, letting out a growl and then came back down onto its front paws. It came down the opposite side of the stream toward him and then tested the depth of the water with one paw, but finding no bottom it brought the paw back again and Will saw the big front claws and how they dug at the soil, then the animal reversed again, coming even with him. Only the depth of the pool and a hesitancy on the bear's part kept the big grizzly from Will.

He had the pack now and he brought it up, slipped one arm after the other through the straps. He bent and lifted the rifle. The bear still had not moved, except to raise its nose some more, tasting the air. Even the sight of the rifle did not seem to deter it. It growled again and showed its yellow teeth, strings of saliva now seen suspended from its upper jaw as it held open a mouth that could easily swallow Will's head whole.

Will bent again, never taking his eyes from the bear, and gathered the rabbits to him. He cleaned the blade of the knife on their fur and then replaced it in the scabbard he kept on his belt. When he was done he came forward to the edge of the water and, still wary of the bear, he separated one of the jackrabbit carcasses and tossed it, spinning end over end, across the pool where it landed in the brush just a few feet from the grizzly.

By the time the bear found the rabbit, Will was already backing up the rock and into the underbrush that lined the stream on all sides. Only when the branches closed around him did he turn and begin to walk up and away from the stream. No sound except that of the water rolling farther down, and even when he had gone another hundred yards or so and turned back, focusing again on the stream and the woods surrounding him, he could hear nothing but the water farther on. For a minute, he kept his eyes fixed on the path he had taken. The far cry of a loggerhead shrike sounded to his right, the bird launched from its perch and dipped through the trees until it broke into open grasslands beyond.

Will followed the bird out, soon moving fast through the grass, pausing to glance back at the belt of wood that followed the stream before he went on again. Not until he had arrived at the small cabin, set the rabbits down, taken the pack from his back and then gone back out to the overlook that faced to the north and the mountains there, did he give himself a little time to pause.

He carried with him the Remington, and looking over the country now, he gathered the strap in his hands, flipped up the scope cover, and brought the rifle to his shoulder, the lens to his eye. He ran the scope along the far edge of the forest to where he knew the stream ran another half mile on. The wind was in the tops of the trees and it worked through the field of Junegrass below, appearing to Will like waves on a great golden lake.

He dropped the rifle from his shoulder and stood looking over the forest and hills, the mountain farther on. He said to himself, "Just 'cause you don't see him don't mean he's not out there."

Will thought of the big buck he had seen in the lightning storm, he thought of the beaver lodge and the hole dug in the side. He knew what the bear was doing down here. He knew why the bear had come.

THREE HOURS LATER, AFTER HE HAD FINISHED SKINNING THE rabbits and packing the meat in salt, he came up out of the root cellar and looked toward the distant beating stars above, the waning moon behind the trees. He had eaten and then gone about his work. He would give the rabbits, along with several other critters he had snared or shot in the weeks past, to the people they were owed to, the people he worked for and who in some way had set him up in this life when he'd thought his life had been over.

The skins they would sell, too. Most of the money went to the church, but some of it came back to Will. Money for supplies like snare wire, .308 rifle cartridges, butter, flour, and other supplies Will could not readily take from the woods. He was careful with everything, knowing each and every item, and their exact measure, within his cabin and down in the root cellar, as if each were recorded on a piece of paper and not just stored away in his head.

He looked now around the small camp he kept and the house he had been made ward of in those first years of Eden's Gate. The fire he had made earlier to cook his meal of biscuits still showed the small red glow of coals at its center. The night now fully upon him as he walked the short distance to the fire, blew the gray ash from atop the beating coals and then piled fresh kindling atop.

For an hour, he sat by the fire and thought about the bear. He thought about how easily the bear could have killed him that day.

TWO DAYS LATER HE FOUND THE WHITE CHURCH TRUCK WAITING for him when he came up the hill. Will carried behind him a field-dressed buck on a travois he had constructed himself. He stood sweating in place under the gambrel he used for skinning deer and elk. The travois he'd made from two long poles he'd cut from within an aspen growth, lashed crossways with smaller branches and then tied all together with paracord. It had made it easier to bring his kill the two miles from where he'd shot the buck, but it had not made it easy.

He stood watching the truck and looking around at the little clearing his cabin sat within, but he saw nothing other than the truck to suggest anyone else was here. Tired from his efforts he coughed and set down the buck, then he walked to the cold ash of the firepit and spit down among the dead coals. Looking now on the buck behind him, the antlers like a crown of thorns and those black, mirrorlike eyes looking back at him, he was unsure whether he should begin his skinning or go out in search of the owner of the truck.

By the time Will had taken the rifle from his shoulder and placed the pack on the ground, Lonny had come up out of the root cellar with the rabbits. He was beside the truck, lifting the lid on a cooler and then dropping the rabbits inside with the rest of the meat when he saw Will standing there.

"I see you've kept busy the last three weeks," Lonny said, looking down at the coolers and then back up at Will. Lonny wore a trucker's cap on his head. He was bearded like all members of the church were and his two snake tattoos emerged from the sleeves of his T-shirt and coiled down his forearms to the backs of each hand.

"I thought you'd be here tomorrow," Will said, glancing around the clearing, wondering if Lonny was alone.

"Something came up."

"What kind of something?"

"The kind that made me think of you." Lonny smiled and then walked the ten or so paces from where the truck sat to where Will was standing. "I got you a little job you can do for us."

"I like the job I got now."

Lonny circled and looked at the buck. He made a low whistling sound and then clucked his tongue. "He's a beaut."

"Should be about seventy-five pounds of usable meat once I get him skinned and bone him out."

"You going to keep the head?"

"I was thinking about putting it up inside."

Lonny stared at him. He ran the tip of his tongue across his upper lip and then inside over his gums. He picked something from his teeth and flicked it away. "That rack would make a nice present for John or The Father."

"I shot him through the heart. Meat should be good still. Just have to get him up on the hook and get to work."

Lonny smiled. "You have a pretty nice thing going on out here. Don't go thinking we haven't forgotten that."

Will looked Lonny over. The man was six foot, nearly as tall as Will, but skinny and lean. Those two forearms with the snake tattoos were all muscle and sinew and not much else. Will had heard Lonny could use them, too. Though he'd never seen the man hurt anyone, he had heard stories. A few saying how Lonny could strike out with each fist fast as any rattlesnake might bite.

"It'll take me about twenty minutes to skin and bone out the deer. Then another hour to clean up the sinew and separate the muscle groups. You got that time?"

"Just skin it and throw it in the back of the truck. There's plenty at Eden's Gate who can help with the meat. And keep the head on."

Will brought up his empty canteen and crossed to the house, dipped the canteen into the bucket of water, watching the bubbles come up until it was full. He stood drinking from the canteen and then dipped it again. When he walked back over to Lonny and the buck, Lonny was looking the rifle over.

"You shoot a .308?"

"Yes."

"That big enough for a grizzly?"

Will waited. He didn't like the way this was heading.

Lonny took a small pouch from his pocket, pinched some tobacco and started to roll a cigarette with papers he'd taken from the same pouch. "We got us a problem and I think you're the guy to solve it for us." He finished the cigarette and placed it between his lips. "You want one?"

Will declined and then walked around to the deer to undo the paracord from where he had tied it to secure the buck. He heard the flick of the lighter, then the exhale of the smoke and by the time the paracord had been taken from the haunches and underbelly of the deer, Will was smelling cigarette smoke and not much else.

"You know the Kershaw place out on two twenty-four?"

"I know the Kershaws. Their place is about twenty miles from here." He knelt and, taking the knife from his belt, made a small hole between each of the deer's knees and rear tendons. Next he got the hook from the gambrel and hoisted the deer up so that it was swinging, spraddle-legged, in front of him. "They still raise cattle?"

"You'd likely know this if you came to The Father's Sunday sermons. Being there as little as you are, you think no one notices when you miss one. But I notice. And I guess now I'll be the one to tell you the church took over the operation a few weeks ago."

"Took over?"

"Made some improvements." Lonny smoked. He walked off a way and looked down at the field below. When he came back, he said, "I'd like you to hunt and kill a big grizzly that took down a heifer there yesterday."

Will stopped the careful job he was doing with the skin, working with the knife to bring it down off the haunches. He looked over at Lonny. "You're asking me to look past a heap of laws and regulations."

"That's what you do, isn't it? You think we have you set up here on church land so you can pick and choose?"

Will didn't like being talked to that way. It was true, maybe he did have it good out here. Fighting with Lonny wasn't going to do him any favors. "You have a plan?"

"That's why I'm here."

"Grizzlies are scavengers," Will said. "They're opportunistic. You'll never know how to read them, how to understand them. They'll hunt and kill their own young if they have to. They're survivors. This bear you want me to kill, he may have just been passing through. He might just have seen the heifer and gone for it. He might be miles away by now."

"And if he isn't?"

"We could go to jail for this. You understand that, right?"

"What happens on our land is our business."

Will sucked at the inside of his cheeks. The bloody knife hung in his hand and he let his eyes roll across the clearing in which his cabin sat. He could see no way out of this. "When I was over in Vietnam there was a tiger that used to hunt and kill the men stationed at my base. They tried damn near everything they could to kill it. But it always came back. No one ever saw it. The animal might as well have been a ghost. We found paw prints, we found blood trails, but we never saw it."

"And you killed it?"

"No," Will said. "How do you kill something you cannot see?"

Lonny finished the cigarette and flicked it away toward the firepit. "You think this bear is supernatural? You think this bear is some heavenly retribution? The Father would love that. That would be scripture to the man."

"No," Will said. "I'm saying I don't know a goddamn thing. I'm saying I can't help you."

"Now, Will. You know that's not something you can say." Lonny took a small flask from his pocket, worked the top off and then drank. He never took his eyes from Will. "You need a little liquid encouragement?"

"No," Will said.

Lonny took another swig of the flask and then he sat on one of the cut logs by the firepit and looked up at Will. "Things could be a lot worse for you," Lonny said. "Being out here as much as you are you haven't seen the things that I've seen. You don't know what they have us doing these days."

"The Father chose to put me here," Will said.

"The Father says the time is approaching."

"Is that right?"

"He tells us to read the signs. Plain as day, he says. All hell is breaking loose out East. And it's coming, all the goddamn way across the country. I see you, Will. I see how you are. You're not a believer like the new blood we have now, but you will be. You will be one of these days and you're going to need to be saved like all the rest of us."

"I see you over there keeping the faith," Will said, looking at the flask and the man that held it.

"Old habits die hard."

"Yes, they do."

Lonny took another drink. He ran his eyes out to the clearing and the view of the mountains farther on. Insects were dancing in the last lowering rays of sun. "What happened to the tiger?"

"The powers that be went and talked to the local villagers. A pit was suggested. The enemy used to use them on us. Just slaughter us all to hell. Maybe you've heard about it? Lines of sharpened sticks, covered over by a latticework of twigs and then concealed. Gravity did the rest." Will worked the knife across the skin again, yanking the hide down until he reached the front legs, then he worked the blade down along the backs of each, cutting and pulling.

"That's how you got the tiger?"

"No, the tiger waited. He took one man out at a time. He waited in that jungle and he watched and he knew without a doubt that we were there to kill him and we never did."

"What the fuck." Lonny took another drink. "Why the fuck did you tell me that story in the first place?"

"Sometimes it's important to understand you don't always get what you want."

"That goes both ways," Lonny said. He looked Will's work over and then he got up to leave. "You better throw that fucker in the back of the truck for me. I've got a lot to do before I start digging us a hole out by the Kershaw place."

"You're not going to catch him," Will said.

"Yeah, well, I'm going to do everything I goddamn can. And you're going to help me."

WILL STOPPED AND STOOD IN THE SAME SPOT HE'D SEEN THE bear stand to meet the coming thunderstorm. He turned and looked up on his place. The slant of the roof, the tin cap of the stovepipe, the whole cabin almost part of the forest itself, so small and nondescript atop the little hill.

A day had passed since Lonny had come and Will now carried three beavers on a string. He had shot them from the shore that morning and then watched them bob to the surface. Stripping down naked, he'd gone wading into the pond until his feet lost the bottom. For a little while, after he'd gathered them up and come back to the shore, he glanced back at the lodge there and the hole in it that the bear had torn a few days before. Blood and water now dripped down his naked forearm and fell in a splatter to the mud below. He gutted each animal to preserve the meat longer and then tied the castor glands shut.

The Kershaw place was twenty miles away, but it was half that if he cut through the forest and made his way through the fields. It was getting on in the afternoon, and as he stood in the place the bear had stood he tried to think the bear's thoughts, see the bear's path, and know the bear's world.

HE DREAMT AND HIS MIND WANDERED IN TIME AND HIS UNCONscious thoughts were of old stories he'd heard as a kid, passed down through his family all the way back to the pioneer days. Bears twice the height of a man, miners and loggers hunting them near to extinction. Ranch owners shooting any they saw. These bears simply hungry, simply doing what they could to survive, and doing it the only way they knew how.

He woke in the night and sat up, looked about the clearing he had chosen to make his camp. The Kershaw place was another five miles or so. The camp made when he had come up the ridge and moved into the high country gave him a vantage over the land. And while the setting sunlight spread like an orange dye through the darkening blue water of the sky, he ate mountain blueberries he'd gathered and chewed bits of smoked jerky he'd made from past kills. Fifty yards away the beavers hung from a branch on a tree and while he took his meal he watched the way the coming night breeze turned the carcasses. The flat, broad tails like some sort of sail catching the wind.

It was to this string that he looked now, fresh from his dreams, watching the dark shapes of the beavers turn in the blue starlight. He coughed and spit away mucus and in the silence that followed, his eyes roamed the clearing considering each tree and blade of grass as if each harbored some unknown threat to his person.

In the east a pale red light shone like that of the sun in primordial dawn, but he knew it was not. He stood now, folding his wool blanket away, then pulling one boot on after the other. He reached for the rifle and then set out across the clearing, moving through grass that came to his kneecaps.

When he reached the far wood, he could smell the smoke. And by the time he'd gone a hundred yards farther in, passing through dappled shadows and pools of moonlight beneath the overhead evergreen thatch, he had begun to hear the chanting and the calls of the worshippers below. After another hundred yards, he came to a broad rock face that ran for a quarter mile to either side of him and outlined the river valley below. A river ran at the bottom of the rock face, the water black and ink-like but the light of the fire shining in places where it caught on the surface. Farther on he could see the great bonfire. The pile of wood was ten feet high and the fire burning another twenty or thirty feet in the air. He could feel the thermals working out over the river and then rise, a vortex of warmth and cool river air swirling like a whirlpool before him.

The bonfire cast its light all around in the circle that formed at its base and in this Will saw the shapes of those who had come to worship its destruction. The sound of their chanting heard as they prayed and worshipped, their heads bent in a chaotic dance of their own making. The words, at this distance, not clear to him as they bounced off the rock face and were lost in the thermal wind. But Will had heard them before and knew much of what was being said, though he liked not to think of it. They were part of the Eden's Gate Church, and like Lonny had said, they did what they pleased and worshipped in ways of their own choosing. For this was their land and whether Will liked it or not he had come to them twelve years before looking for salvation, and they in turn had given it to him, making him what he was now, game warden, poacher, killer of beasts large and small.

Keeping back from the ledge a little he found a shadowed bit of rock and, putting the rifle on the forty or so people that danced and circled below, he flipped up the scope cover and began to roam his eye across those below. Many wore the white robes of the church. He ran the scope from the bearded faces of men to the unkempt, flowing hair of the women. He watched not just them but the elongated shadows of their movements, the shadows of legs and arms cast across the fiery ground like some sort of transmogrified creature, half beast and half man.

By the time he had run the scope all the way around the circle they were forming into a line that stretched from the burning pile of wood down toward the river. Taking his eye from the scope, he moved forward on his elbows until he was at the edge of the cliff. He reached back, brought up the rifle and, careful not to let the light catch on the glass lens, he looked down on the figure of The Father there in the river. Fifty-some years old, he wore the same unmoving face that could be terror or salvation to any who looked upon it. The man stood knee-deep in the water in his own robe. The water clung to the material and climbed its way to his chest where it hung from him and showed the strong musculature of his body. He chanted and looked to the heavens and one at a time he invited each worshipper to come to him as he dipped them into the river and held them there, watching as their arms flailed for some sort of purchase.

After all had been baptized a new group was gathered. Some in robes but many in their own clothes, brought huddled together from out of the shadows, some shivering, some visibly frightened. All of them led by men carrying guns and several with machetes. As they walked, the rest of the willing in their baptismal robes closed in behind them, encircling them there on the shore. Out of this group, holding a large revolver, was John Seed, the younger brother of The Father, slighter in build, but cut from the same cloth. Both bearded and tattooed, and both with those all-seeing eyes that seemed to search through the dark with a kind of nocturnal prowess.

With the revolver John went into the water and stopped no more than a few feet from The Father. They waited, the two of them, as men bearing rifles and machetes brought these new worshippers out to them. Each, as had been done with the willing, were baptized in turn and then led back to shore by their guards. And though Will had seen baptisms before, he had not seen anything like this, where men and women were forcibly dipped. Lonny had told him of the shift, and had Will not skipped so many sermons in the past— his own faith waning little by little—Will might not have been as surprised at what he saw down below.

Many on shore were crying and he could see the visible shaking of their shoulders and the terror of the night in their faces. He watched them as if seeing them from out of some bubble that no sound could escape. Their distance and the rush of the water sucking away at the cries they made and the protests they had for this forced ceremony.

For a time he kept the scope on them, watching as they came to the water, tried to fight, to break free from their captors, but none made it far and each met the same fate that had awaited those baptized before them.

Years had gone by since Will had been a part of this. And none of it had been as it was now, watching those down there who were unwilling. In those times, years before, he had seen the giving of a soul and the baptizing of many. He had stood in a robe on the side of a river like this one and he had done his part to be one of them, giving his soul to the church. But that even seemed like another life, another time, a past that had grown distant from the man he was now and the role he'd been given.

Having seen enough, he pulled back from the edge. He stood and moved away toward the forest and then from out of the depths he heard the crack of a shotgun. He rushed to the edge and looked down. He could see many among them had cowered, the guards standing above them. Still farther back stood many of the first of the willing and in the water waited The Father, and John. Will could not tell who had fired the shot and he ran his eyes down the river, wondering if he might see a body pulled toward the rapids and then out of sight where the river curved away farther on.

But he saw no body and when he brought his eyes back to The Father, the man was already calling for the next to be baptized. And Will, as witness in all of this, looked again to the empty place in the river where the rapids turned the water to white, and he was unsure of what he had seen. He let his eyes linger there and he watched how the water ran below him. He thought about the meaning of the baptism and the washing of the sins.

When all had dipped their heads beneath the water, Will moved away from the edge. He did not need to know what The Father would say to them now. He did not need to watch anymore. For he knew this part well, he had heard it twelve years before when he had come willing to the church and he repeated it to himself as he walked back to his camp. "We stand on the edge of a great chasm. Below us is the fate of mankind. Humanity has grown numb to the machine of strife that it has created, but *we cannot*. We and we alone have been chosen to survive this calamity and rebuild. We are all angels, and we few are set on a path back to the garden. We are a Family. I am your Father. You are my Children. And together we will march to Eden's Gate."

THE MORNING MIST WAS IN THE FIELDS BEYOND WHEN WILL came to the top of the small rise and looked down upon the Kershaw house. The grassy fecal odor of the cattle lingered in the air. He ran his eyes out along the cattle wire until it dropped away over the edge of the rounded field. A slim line of wood smoke escaped the chimney top and this too he watched.

Moving now, following the gravel road that ran the top of the hill, he came down through stands of pine and could see the barn below. One of the broad doors stood open, its lowermost corner resting in the dirt. Dark shadows seen within. And though he could smell the cows in the air he had not seen one and he stepped closer, wondering now what had happened and whether the bear had come again and would now emerge from within that greater shadow, covered in the fresh blood of some new slaughter.

He found nothing of the sort, simply hay and the chipped paint of the stalls. The heady aroma of forgotten animals, long vacated from this place. When he came out again he saw the white church truck parked off the road, closer to the pine forest than to the house. A shovel and pick had been leaned against the side of the bed with two yellow cowhide gloves resting atop each pole, like the coxcomb beginnings of some makeshift pair of scarecrows.

Fifty yards away the opening of the screen door startled Will. He turned and looked toward the porch where Lonny now waited, dragging his fingers through his beard and looking across the grass and gravel to Will.

When Will walked up, Lonny had already taken his pouch from one of his pockets and had begun to roll a cigarette. He stood atop the porch. He wore a thin cotton tank that clung tight around his ribcage all the way to the waist of his pants. His hair was mussed and on the skin of his face were the visible imprints of sleep. He spat and then wet his lips and he watched Will where he stood with the beavers on a string over one shoulder and the rifle on the other.

"You sleeping here?" Will asked.

"Sometimes."

Will watched him rummage through his pocket and then bring up the lighter. Lonny cupped the lighter and brought the flame to his lips, the cigarette flared and the first draught of smoke was taken down within his lungs. All of it seen in a kind of deliberate and slow catharsis, smoke and air, the shift of a breeze, the washing of the smoke across his skin. The smell of the smoke commingled with the smell of the cows now made their absence from this place more apparent. "What happened to the cattle?"

"Eaten," Lonny said.

Will looked past him to where the door stood open, as if the cows might somehow be within. "And the Kershaws?"

"Gone."

"Gone?"

Lonny was smiling a little, watching Will, and then he leaned and spat again, not even bothering to get the spittle off the porch.

WILL LEFT THE BEAVERS ON THE KITCHEN COUNTER AND WENT to use the bathroom. When he was done he came back into the small hallway that ran out from the living room. His hands were wet from washing them in the sink and he ran his palms down his shirt-front then flipped them over and ran the backs against the material, drying them one side at a time like the stropping of a razor across the leather of a belt.

Across the hallway was a partially closed bedroom door and he pushed it open and looked within. A queen-sized bed, the sheets pulled back on each side. Two pillows and the indents of two heads, as if whoever had been here had simply risen minutes before and now was out walking the field or waiting on the coffee to finish percolating.

He turned and went farther down the hallway, moving away from the kitchen and living room. He came to two more bedrooms, pushed each door open in turn and glanced inside. In one, blue walls and the hanging models of airplanes built from some kit. In the other, pink walls and a dresser lined along its top with stuffed animals and small plastic toy horses, many toppled over, but some still standing in various poses of action like a frozen moment captured by a child's diorama.

"I heard you had a daughter." Lonny stood at the head of the hallway, thirty paces away.

"You heard?"

"That's what they told me. That's what they said when they gave me the job of watching over you."

Will took in the pink color of the walls, the diffuse curtains across the single window. He'd had a daughter. He'd had a wife. A family. Will had had a whole life before this one and it was his fault his wife and daughter were not with him anymore, that they were not part of this world anymore. And though he had come to The Father and to Eden's Gate for some kind of forgiveness, he knew now that forgiveness was not what he'd found.

He closed his eyes a moment. He smelled dust and something

beneath it all that was sweet and almost recognizable. When he opened his eyes again, he turned and looked toward Lonny. "What happened here?" Will asked.

"YOU'RE PART OF US, WILL. BUT WHEN YOU, OR JOHN, OR THE Father, or even I look at the same thing it does not mean we see the same thing." They walked the field. The blood could still be seen in the grass where the cow had died, where the bear had come and eaten its fill and then moved on again. "Every one of us has our purpose. You have lived out there and you have served the purposes of the church and they are grateful for it."

"And the Kershaws?" Will asked, still thinking of the empty rooms and what had been said to him. The answer Lonny had given that was not an answer.

"They served their purpose, too. Just as you do, or I do. Each of us a servant."

"And your purpose?" Will asked. He knelt now, looking out across the field, retracing the steps of the bear, seeing it in his mind. The big loping slide and pull of its muscle as it ran, the sheen of its fur seen beneath the light of the sun and the way the dust of the pasture and earth beneath its great claws would have risen, kicked into the air.

"I make sure The Father and the church receive their due."

"Is that what they are calling it now?"

"We are a community. As you know well enough, if the church helps you, you are expected to pay that kindness back."

"And the Kershaws paid?"

"Until they could not anymore."

"And now?"

"They have been repurposed."

Will rose and walked toward where the fence had been bent. He could see in the packed dirt and the close-cropped grass, the indents and scuffle of the bear's movements. "Were the Kershaws here when this happened?"

"They were. But they were already at their end. They had already slaughtered many of their cows to feed the church and their time here and their hold on this place was coming to an end."

Will looked now to the surrounding wood. He thought of all he'd seen. He thought of the bear out there. He wondered if it was there still. If it watched them even now. "I saw The Father last night," Will said. "I saw John. I saw the baptism in the river."

"It is not just the Kershaws that owe a debt to the church. Many in this community have been helped. They have had their mortgages paid. They have had their debts forgiven. They have suckled at the teat of Eden's Gate," Lonny said, a wicked smile now breaking from his lips. "And the church and The Father only ask their due, whether that is the slaughter of a cow, or the growing of a crop, or the giving of their soul to Eden's Gate."

"Some did not give their soul as freely as the others."

Lonny laughed. "Some give more freely than others, but in the end they all will give."

Will thought of the girl's room. He thought about the past. He thought about how one drink led to another. He thought of another life altogether. Finally, he said, "In the church there is salvation."

"You're getting it now," Lonny said. "And here I was starting to think you'd forgotten."

•　•　•

THE BEAR PIT HAD BEEN DUG AT THE EDGE OF THE WOOD. THE
roots cleanly cut and a thatch of thin pine had been woven to cover
it all. At the bottom of the pit, thick, straight branches had been
sharpened and then dug into the ground with their points toward
the sky. Will looked it over and then, when he was satisfied, he
brought the beavers out from the house and using a knife he cut
away the string he'd used to tie off the castor glands.

"Did you have help with this?" Will asked, working to get the
beavers hung on a thin metal wire that would span the opening of
the pit.

"John came with a few of his men and they helped to dig the pit
and then when it was done we sharpened the sticks and set them
out below. He was quite impressed with your design."

"You told him about the tiger?"

"I left out some parts."

"Like how the tiger killed anyone who tried to hunt it?"

"Something like that," Lonny said.

Will walked the edge of the pit, the wire trailing behind him.
He came to a broad tree trunk and tied one end of the wire there.

"This is going to work?" Lonny asked.

Will looked to where Lonny was standing, his eyes on the wire
and the beavers that waited there in the dirt. Will brought up one
of the beavers and held it tail-end toward Lonny. "What do you
smell?" he asked, holding the beaver still and watching as Lonny
bent slightly, then his eyes raised on Will.

"Sweet? Almost like Christmas cookies?"

"It's vanilla," Will said. "There's a gland here that smells and
even tastes just like vanilla. The old-time trappers used to sell
it. Sometimes they still do. Read the label on a box of cookies
next time you're at the store. I believe they list this stuff as natural
flavoring."

"You're fucking with me."

"I wish I was."

"And bears like this stuff?"

"They love this stuff." Will tied the other end of the wire to a tree on the opposite side of the pit and pulled the wire tight, suspending the beavers up over the center of the pit. "Like a fly to shit."

"Or a bear to beaver ass," Lonny said.

FOR AN HOUR, AFTER THEY HAD FINISHED, THEY SAT AT THE EDGE of the porch on dining room chairs they'd dragged from inside. Lonny smoked. He picked loose tobacco from his teeth and from his lips and flicked it away. He leaned forward with his forearms resting across his thighs, the cigarette dangling from his fingers. Mostly he watched the edge of the wood where the pit had been dug. He ran his eyes to the far mountains and at times he held out a hand and called for the rifle, putting the scope to his eye and searching through the deep shadows of the forest, or raising the barrel on the mountains so far away.

"You think he's out there?" Lonny asked, handing the rifle back to Will.

"He's out there," Will answered. The forestock was warm where Lonny had held it. Will put the scope to his eye and looked through the glass, then brought the rifle back down again.

"What makes you so confident?"

"He has to be somewhere, doesn't he?"

Lonny shook his head. "I don't know how you can do this every day, just sit here like this and wait for something to chance out from between the trees," he said, standing now. "I found a few liquor bottles the Kershaws had tucked away. You want any to pass the time?"

"You ever wonder what would happen if John or The Father came along and found you breaking their rules?"

"We all have our secrets," Lonny said. "Every one of us."

WILL WAITED. HE WATCHED LONNY TAKE DRINK AFTER DRINK and then watched the man curl up on the couch mumbling to himself with the bottle still in hand. Within five minutes there was the sound of his snoring.

Out in the field the light had started to go and the insects danced in the air, a few zigzagging in the last of the light, while others zoomed past like they had somewhere more important to be. He watched them for a time and he watched the place in the woods where the pit was, then he turned from the window and walked down the hall to the first bedroom.

He sat on the bed and looked about the place. A woman's nightgown hung by a hook close by the door. The material thin and white, the sleeves very short and an intricate stitching at the edges of each that ran out and down and across at the chest. For a while he sat and studied it like some sort of mystery to be solved.

The light had gone out of the sky now and the whole room had grown dark. He ran his eyes over the place and took in the twin dressers and the mirror across the room. A single chair sat in a corner with a laundry basket on it, filled almost all the way to the brim with clothes that looked to be both female and male.

When his eyes came back around on the nightgown he did not know that he would do it until he did. He rose from his seat on the bed, took down the nightgown and held it in his hands. His wife had had one like this once. And though he had trained himself not to think about her, or his daughter, he thought of them now.

He brought the nightgown close to his face. He smelled laven-
der and dirt and something he thought maybe was sunscreen. He
held the gown away from him now and he went to the bed and laid
it in the place he thought that it went. Then he rounded the bed
and sat for a while, telling himself this was all craziness, that if John
or The Father walked in right now, they would know he had not
been saved as he had said he was in that long ago time, and that
what had troubled him then, still troubled him now, and no salvation by church or The Father could give him respite.

WHEN HE WOKE IN THE MORNING THE GOWN LAY ON THE BED
beside him. He reached out a hand toward it and felt of the material and for a moment wished there to be flesh and blood there
beside him. He thought of the woman who had been his wife and
he thought of the life that had been his own. He closed his eyes and
that's when he heard the soft barking of what could have been a dog
pup, but what Will knew was a bear.

Lonny was still asleep on the couch, the bottle fallen from his
hand when Will came out of the room. The rifle was still where
Will had laid it after coming in off the porch. He took it now, raised
it on the pit at the edge of the forest, and looked through the scope.
One beaver was missing from the wire and the thatch that covered
the trap had been sprung.

Quickly he took the rifle from his shoulder, fingered back the
bolt until he could see the bullet in the chamber. He slid the bolt
back up into place, pushed the safety forward and now he looked
about the room for his pack and the ammo he knew was within.
When he found the pack and had pulled it on over his shoulders,
he went out onto the porch into the morning light.

Again, he put the scope on the pit trap then ran his eye along the edge of the forest. Everything was as it had been before, except for the one beaver and the latticework covering that had hid the spikes below.

When the barking came again to his ear he knew what they had caught was not the big boar grizzly he had seen in the rain. No, this was not that. He came down off the porch and, as quick and silent as he could, he crossed through the field and came to the place the pit had been dug and looked down.

The bear was a female grizzly and Will knew now why the big boar had come down from the mountains, hungry and following the mother and cub. When Will looked up at the forest there was no sign of the cub he knew there to be. The silence of the place was now full and complete and the cub may be on the run, but most likely hiding. Down in the pit the mother bear lay dead. The spikes seen in places where they had punctured her body and come up through her skin. The sharpened white of the wood now tinged red with her blood.

Will crossed now, moving around one side of the pit trap. There in the dirt at his feet was the imprint of the mother's paw. Close by, almost erasing that of its mother, the cub's prints could be seen where it had moved back and forth along the edge of the pit, calling for its mother and waking Will from his sleep.

By the size of the paw print he could see the cub was no more than a few months old and that, as he followed one print after another, it had moved up and away from the field. The path moving in a somewhat direct line toward the roadway above.

He took several steps this way and then turned back to the trap. Two beavers still hung by the wire. He reached and undid one end of the wire and brought the two carcasses down. With the beavers in hand he went back to the small paw prints he'd found and went up the hill in a careful study of the surrounding landscape, watching for movement, listening for sound.

His movements were slow and deliberate. His watchfulness had less to do with startling the cub and more to do with what that cub might have already drawn from the forest. For Will knew it was not just him that was hunting this cub, but likely the larger, boar grizzly.

When he came to the road he could see where the small cub had run across the gravel and Will marked the front paws and then looked for the broad back paws of each foot and the way they had pushed and swept at the gravel. He crossed, looking at each paw print then went down into the forest at the other side of the road and continued, following the prints, sometimes losing them, sometimes taking his direction from a broken twig or a tuft of hair found caught on the rough bark of a pine.

He was two hours in his tracking and by the time he came to the thicket of elderberry the sun had risen high in the sky and the forest had begun to steam from the heat. Will stopped. He had carried the rifle in his hand for the entirety of his search. Now he set it aside and knelt, looking down at the fresh paw print the cub had left in the mud. The whole of the thicket seeming to follow the low depression of a waterway Will could not yet see.

As he stood up, he was almost certain something had moved within the thicket. Without taking up the rifle, he inched forward. He could see now the dark muddied front paws of the cub, and farther up, just where they disappeared within the bush, he saw the brown, almost blond fur of its summer coat.

Not wanting to take his eyes from the spot, he reached and felt for one of the beavers and then once he had the carcass in his hand, he threw it forward. Will waited and watched. The snout emerged, black and pasted with mud, as the bear cub reached with its teeth, first testing the meat, then pulling it back within the thicket, placing one paw atop the carcass to hold it in place as it began to tear at the flesh. All the while keeping an eye on Will where he squatted.

When the cub had chewed the beaver to the white bone, Will reached again and found the second beaver. This time using his knife to quarter it, he threw one piece close to the bear, then a second a little more than a foot from the thicket. When the bear cub had finished the first quarter of it Will watched it come forward, moving low to the ground to gather the second quarter of meat and then lay eating it, still watching Will.

"You were hungry," Will said, his voice no more than a whisper. The bear turned toward him with its ears cupped and focused in his direction.

He held out another quarter and waited, not putting the beaver meat down on the ground, but instead holding it outward in his hand, the way one might try to steady the nerves of a long-lost dog that had found its way to the wild. When the bear cub came forward and nipped at the meat Will did not let go, forcing the bear to inch closer. The cub a good hundred pounds and possibly more, already showing much of the muscle of an adult grizzly, and the claws that curved and dug up the earth almost like teeth. By the time it had worked up enough confidence to grab the meat from Will's hand, Will had already begun to wonder how far the cub would be willing to follow him.

THERE WAS LITTLE BUT ASH AND A FEW BLACKENED PIECES OF wood remaining in the place of the fire. Will looked to the river then back down to where the slight breeze off the water turned the ash over and over again, running it now in a dusting across the land. He walked to the river's edge and saw in the river mud where the worshippers had stood. Scanning across the water, he tried to find the place on the high rock face where he had stood watching, but there were many places and many shadows. He turned away from the river and went up again along the wash to where the fire had burned. The bear cub was there, pawing at a half-burnt piece of wood.

When he approached the bear cub shied away, then came back little by little. A couple hours had passed and Will often lost the cub, but waiting, soon would see the small bear loping through fields, or weaving between the trunks of the pine forest at a distance no less than a hundred feet away.

At the height of his climb up out of the depression where the church had held their bonfire he found he was disappointed not to see the bear climbing up behind him. But when he walked back a hundred feet he could see the bear running at the side of the river, playing in the shallow water, pausing to drink, and then running again. He called to the bear and soon the bear had come up out of the river.

Two hours later when he came up the rise toward his cabin, the bear was no more than twenty feet behind him. As he came into the small clearing before his place, the bear hesitated, standing there like it had come up against a very real, but very invisible wall that surrounded the clearing and the cabin within. The animal paced back and forth and then called out to him, making that low barking sound. Will walked back to it and held out his hand, watching as the bear pushed its nose forward now, smelling his skin then pushing at his hand until Will raised it ever so and began to scratch away at the side of the bear's face like they had done this intimate appraisal of each other a thousand times before.

• • •

WHEN HE WOKE THE NEXT DAY, WILL FED THE BEAR CUB AND then, as was his custom, he set out with his snares and pack, carrying his rifle while his hat shaded his eyes against the rising sun. He walked down the rise and out along the field, the cub following, loping behind, often pausing to bite at the tender tips of grass. When Will passed on into the belt of trees that lined the stream beyond, the bear came crashing after him. The two of them now came to the edge of the stream to drink and to dip paws and hands within the moving water.

Many of the snares had been slipped, and Will went one by one looking each over and then resetting them. Twice, in the place he had set a snare there was only the blood and hair of a rabbit left to find. The bear cub sniffing at the ground, running its nose toward the higher field.

"Coyote is my guess," Will said. His eyes up as he searched for clues as to where he might find his snare. Then moving in concentric circles, he widened his search until he found the place the rabbit had been carried and then eaten. The remains no more than a collection of bones and tufts of hair, but the wire snare not far off.

By the time he had circled and reset his snares it was midafternoon and he walked back across the Junegrass field with the bear trailing, running then pausing, just as it had before.

When he came to the rise that led toward his cabin the bear cub was still at play there in the field. The sun now ahead of him as Will walked, his shadow behind, stretching away from him down toward the field like his own dark reflection pulled long and thin across the grass.

• • •

THE SOUND OF THE RIFLE SHOT CUT THROUGH THE AIR. WILL dropped to his belly, his fingers gripping the roots and dirt, the smell of the grass flooding his nostrils. It had been forty years since anyone had shot at him, and it had been in another country, in what had, at the time, seemed like another world altogether. But the feeling had not changed, nor had the spike of adrenaline that went coursing down every one of his veins.

Another shot fired but this time it was far overhead and he looked up but all he could see was the Junegrass and the tops of the pines farther on. He heard the clack of the bolt and then the dissonant sound of laughter and the talk of men. He came up on one elbow, turning to look back down into the field where the bear cub had paused, sniffing the air then standing on hind legs, looking his way.

The rifle sounded again and Will heard the cut of the bullet as it tore through the air and then he saw the puff of the dirt appear on the ground just to the side of the bear. He heard a man curse then he heard the clack of the bolt again and Will looked to the bear who now was smelling the place the bullet had struck, as if this were some new game Will had set up for him to play.

Will turned over again, he could not see the men up on the hill but he could hear them and he knew almost without any doubt that they were firing on the bear and they were trying to kill it. Will looked one last time to his cabin, but the sun had grown lower and the rays that flooded down were blinding.

He sat now, knowing in some way he was not the target and he took the rifle from his shoulder and pushed forward the safety then raised the scope to his eyes. The first shot he took sprayed rock and dirt up over the snout of the bear. And the bear, as if knowing Will had betrayed him, now turned to regard Will where he sat on the lowermost part of the hill. Will ejected the casing then loaded another. There were men talking now as they came down the hill, laughing and calling to each other and now calling to Will, but Will did not hear them, and he raised the rifle again, set the sight on the bear, putting crosshairs right over the ear before pulling the trigger. The bullet, as far as he could tell, buzzed right by the ear and set the bear to running.

Just as the bear came to the far belt of trees at the other edge of the meadow it paused and looked back. Will watched it through the scope. He watched the bear taste the air. He watched the eyes roam and settle on Will and the men that now approached from up on the hill. When the next rifle shot sounded, Will could not tell if the bullet had struck home. He saw only that the bear jumped and then, like it had never been there at all, it was gone, passed away from the visible world into the dark thicket of trees that lined the stream farther on.

Will turned and saw John Seed moving down through the grass, a rifle in his hand with a wood stock and bolt-action lever, the gray smoke that came from the barrel curving up and over his shoulder like some sort of serpent. His men, including Lonny, all followed behind. All of them carrying weapons and all spreading outward as they came on Will and now circled him where he sat in the grass, his own Remington rifle held close in his lap.

"You're a man who likes to play at dangerous games," John said as he came up. "I remember how you used to drink. I remember what state you were in when you came and asked us to help you. Are you still that man, Will?"

"No."

"That's good to hear, Will. That's very good to hear. It looked for a moment there like you might have forgotten."

"How did it look?"

"Like maybe you were trying to make friends with the set of fangs that might kill you one day."

Will ran his eyes from John over to Lonny. When he looked back at John he asked if they had found the bear in the pit.

"That's why we came here," John said. "Lonny suggested it. He said you can track just about anything. That true?"

Will moved his eyes to Lonny again. "Since you all set me up at this place, I've hunted nearly everything that walks or crawls on four legs. What is it you're looking for here?"

"We got us a bit of a situation and we'd like you to solve it. You think you could find someone for us?"

"Someone?"

"A girl has gone missing."

"I'm not any kind of detective, if that's what you're asking."

"I'm not asking you to be. I'm asking can you track her through these woods and bring her back in for us?"

"You're asking me to hunt down a human being?"

John smiled. "I'm not really asking."

Once I was lost in the wilderness and as I came to understand the wilderness, I too became wild, and out of this wilderness I was fostered anew, not just as a man, but as an animal, clothed in the blood of my kill, wild in the heart, and with a powerful hunger for all those who would trespass against me and the wilderness I now called my home.

—THE FATHER, EDEN'S GATE
Hope County, Montana

WILL HALF SLID, HALF CLIMBED DOWN ALONG THE SLOPE, following the path of broken branches and flattened leaf matter. The truck was on its side another fifty feet down. He could only see the bottoms of the tires and the metal undercarriage where the drive shaft went straight through from the front of the truck to the back. He carried his pack and wore his hat. He also carried the rifle he used for hunting. It had sat between his legs as he'd come up the mountain, riding shotgun, listening to John tell him which way he'd thought the girl had gone and why.

"You understand we mean to help her?"

"That's why you want to find her?" Will had asked.

"That's why. We want to save her. We want to give her a new life, just like the one we gave to you."

Will looked away out the side of the passenger window. He had his hands resting on the rifle, watching the trees and vegetation blurring past. A deer stood off to the side of the road and he watched it as they passed. He watched it all the way until he couldn't see it anymore and the road had curved away behind them. Will's eyes fell on a tarp in the bed of the truck. One corner coming loose.

"What's back there?" Will asked.

John glanced across to see what Will had seen. "My oldest brother Jacob has been tracking wolves in the mountains nearby. It's some of his equipment."

Will tried to see what was there but the tarp would not stay still.

"The concept is pretty simple," John said. "You hunt one and then tag it with the signal. Once you have one you let it go and then you use the tag to home in on it, and instead of having one, you now can find the whole pack. That's why we need you out there tracking Mary May, Will. We need to bring her back. We need to help her see that she is part of something bigger. We need her to believe as you do, and as I do, that we can help everyone here in this county. Help them to see how strong they can truly be if they could only come together."

"And that works?"

"You know better than I do, Will. You are a hunter. You know that the hunter always uses the best tool he has at hand."

Will thought about what John had said. He slid the remaining fifty feet and came to a stop just before the front axle of the pickup. Above, moving down toward him with a little more caution, Lonny followed, using the thin branches of the currant thicket, that had slowed and must have somewhat cushioned the truck as it went off the road above.

From everything Will had seen thus far it didn't seem at all like they were trying to save the girl. Though Will had seen the baptism and what they might be calling salvation these days.

Moving around the end of the truck he looked at the damage. The front windshield had been cracked and there were fresh scrapes along the metal side panel, one of the headlights had been smashed. Will braced himself against the bumper and rocked the truck a little, thinking that it was very lucky the truck had not rolled the remaining distance through the thicket of currant and crushed itself on the pines farther on. When he lifted himself up and looked down into the cab he could see the passenger side window was completely gone, branches and leaves beneath could be seen where they had been pressed under the weight of the vehicle. There was no blood to be seen and Will let himself back down onto the slope and looked it all over again as if seeing it fresh for the first time.

When Lonny met him there, Will said, "I know this truck."

"I expected you would."

"What are we into here?"

"Damsels in distress," Lonny said, smiling at Will.

"In distress from what?"

"Eternal damnation," Lonny said. "Just like all the rest."

Will gave Lonny one last look then walked his way down along the truck until he came to the tailgate. "They said she went north?"

Lonny came up beside him, carrying his own pack and leaning slightly into the slope as he went, one hand out to brace his movements. "She went this way," Lonny said, pointing to a small opening in the thick green underbrush that could have been an animal track, but that also showed a few small broken branches at chest height.

"They follow her?"

"They followed her as best they could. They said she turned into a goddamn mountain goat just as soon as she hit these woods."

Will turned and looked back up the slope to where the two church trucks sat. John was watching them. "What did John say to you about all this?" Will asked.

"He said only that we should find her. He said she was saying things about the church that just weren't true. He said she's been stirring up the pot back in town, trying to get the sheriff to look into all of us."

"Is there something to look into?"

Lonny shrugged. "You know her, don't you?"

"I know her. I went to school with Mary May's father back when there was a school to go to."

"Then you know how she can be," Lonny said. He looked

up at John now and then glanced back at Will. "We better get to going. John didn't bring the both of us up here so we could sit here jawing."

MARY MAY CAME UP ALONG THE EDGE OF THE DRY AVALANCHE chute, using the slender branches of juniper to pull herself along. She had quit the forest a little while ago and she climbed now in the open. Her breath laboring with the effort, the slick feel of her own sweat down the inside of her shirt. The sun behind her in the west, the heat felt warm against her back, the metal of the .38 feeling solid and heavy beneath the waist of her pants. The gun and a hooded, zippered sweatshirt were all she'd had time to take from the truck before she'd run.

She had lost John and the rest of his men almost five hours before. She climbed now with the alpine breeze, smelling like cracked rock and melted ice, ruffling at the loose fabric of her shirt and teasing out a couple strands of hair that dangled about her face.

Stopping at the base of the ridge she set the .38 to her side then cupped water from a stream and washed it over her face, up along her hair, and then rubbed it along the back of her neck. She drank from between her hands and then stood there looking at the wavering leaves all around, waiting and watching, hoping they were not still out there somewhere trying to follow her.

Satisfied for the moment, she sat there on a large rock and peeled down the jeans she wore to view the dark bruise where her hip had hit the truck door. The bruise purple and black, three quarters up her thigh stretching under the line of her panties and up along her side. She had scrapes in other places, some from when the truck had gone off the road, others from the brush she had been bush-whacking through most of the day.

There had been a thought at one time to head down toward the road but she had given up on it, knowing John was out there, knowing he was looking for her. And that as she had run from the overturned truck, moving through the trees with the sound of the men behind as they crashed through the underbrush after her, she was certain they were not there to offer her any kind of help.

Twenty minutes later she had cut a sharp path to the east and then ducked in behind a big fir tree that lay along the ground, its wide web of roots still clutching at the rocks and dirt that had once surrounded it. She went along the trunk, keeping low, and as she came to the ball of roots and soil she looked back down the mountain to where John and several of his men were standing no more than a hundred feet away. All of them with their weapons. Bearded and tattooed, their eyes searching out the surrounding wood, trying to discern what path they would pursue.

She held the .38 in her hand and her breath when it came seemed louder than she had ever heard it. Though she knew it was only a whisper, that the fear she felt had only made her think it was all the louder.

"Mary May," John called, his eyes roaming now around the surrounding wood. "Come out, come out, wherever you are." He was almost singing and he looked now in the direction of the big windfall fir, but his eyes only passed it by, then continued.

"No one's going to hurt you," John said. He had taken a few steps and she watched the big magnum revolver he held in one hand as he moved, how he ran it one way then another as if it were some form of divining rod and she the precious water. "No one wants this to go any farther than it has to."

She waited. She watched him take a few more steps. His men had already gone ahead of him and he was still looking around. The dark shadows of the forest converged all around him and the great canopy of the trees above.

"You come out and we'll take you to see your brother. We'll take you right to Eden's Gate. We can all be friends. We can all just be one big happy family. You. Your brother. Me. And everyone else, The Father, and all who hear his words."

She watched him till he walked out of sight behind the roots. Then she moved back along the trunk, following him and peeking over to watch where he was going. He spun but she dropped just as fast, her hand still clutching the .38, her face pressed down in the damp forest floor. When she looked again he was another hundred or so feet on, moving in the direction his men had gone. She watched him till she could not see him anymore and then she ran.

A few hours later she had rested at the stream. An hour after that she was climbing the avalanche chute and had come out into the open, using the squat juniper bushes to hold to. Now she came to the top of the windswept ridge and stood there looking down. Steep rock cliffs ran much of the opposite side and stepping closer, she peered now into the dark shadow of a deep abyss. Rock and talus collected three hundred feet below.

She had climbed the ridge hoping to get her bearings, but all she saw was more forest and more hills, mountain after mountain stretching on ahead. Somewhere out there was her brother. All she truly knew about the location of Eden's Gate was that it rested somewhere along the lake farther on. A place that had been scoured out by glaciers millennia ago, the water deep and the mountains and hills that surrounded it running right down into that blue-green water. But it was still very far from where she was. She looked in the direction she thought Eden's Gate might be, scanning the ridge she stood upon then running her eyes down along the far side and out into a river valley far below.

Two or three miles on, on the opposite slope from where she stood, she could see the white dots of animals moving in a mountain field. What she thought at first was a herd of mountain goats, now appeared to her as sheep, and as she studied the surrounding grass she saw a man walk out from the edge of the forest and stand watching the sheep then move back beneath the trees.

She stood and took it all in for the better part of five minutes before she picked her way along the ridge and found a small, gradual chute to descend upon the river valley there below.

WILL KEPT A FEW FEET OUT FROM THE BIG TREE TRUNK AND root ball of the fir. He circled and looked each footfall over. He saw how she had pressed a knee to the ground at one point and how the edges of the depression showed the slight shift of her movements as, he could only guess, she had hidden behind the large trunk and then moved to peer over it at whoever had pursued her.

"What had she been saying?" Will asked.

Lonny turned to look at him. He was standing off a bit in the place Will had gestured for him to go.

"What was she saying to people in town? What made her come out here?"

"Ugly things," Lonny said. "That we were murderers. That we were hiding things, that we were keeping secrets."

"Are we?"

Lonny kept his eyes on Will. He gave a half smile and then

turned to look back the way they'd come, as if John might be standing there. "We haven't done nothing that hasn't needed to be done. You've seen the baptized."

"I've seen it but I'm having a hard time remembering it being done quite that way when the brothers first came up from Georgia," Will said.

"The Father means to cull the herd. He means to separate the weak from those of us who are strong."

"And which is Mary May?"

"You know her, don't you? What would you say?"

"I knew her," Will said. "But that was a long time ago. That was before I came to Eden's Gate. I knew her family, too. And I've seen her brother, Drew, at Eden's Gate, but I haven't spoken more than a few words to him since he joined. I wasn't there when he was baptized and I guess I don't know his story. As a kid Drew always seemed to idolize his daddy, Gary, following him around like he was Gary's own shadow, but Gary was always against Eden's Gate. I guess for Drew that's changed."

"Well," Lonny said. "Things have changed. Things have changed a good deal even from the time I came up here. Even from the time John invited me up here to this place and told me it would be all milk and honey."

"But it hasn't been, has it?"

Lonny looked around at the forest, at the fallen fir tree. "This look like milk and honey to you?" he said. "How long do you think it'll take before we track her down?"

"I'll track her as far as I can. But it doesn't mean we'll find her. She could get down into a riverbed, or she could travel over rock and not leave any trace. Just cause we're looking doesn't mean we'll find her."

"Well which way did she go?"

Will looked up, ran his eyes away from the trunk and out among the trees. "She went this way and it looks like she was running."

"You can tell all that?"

"It's the spacing of the footfalls," Will said, rising now and pointing several out. "Catching up to her is going to be no easy task."

"That right?"

Will walked and kept his eyes down along the ground. He followed Mary May's path up through the forest. The dun of needles displaced here and there where she'd brought a heel down or pushed off with the toe of her shoe.

The last time he'd seen her she had been a teenager, just old enough to work the bar. But that was a long time ago. A very long time since he'd come to the church and gave his soul over to The Father and divorced himself from all he'd known.

MARY MAY CAME ON THEM JUST AS THEY WERE FINISHING THEIR dinner, and one of them rose now to meet her. He walked out to her from under the tree where they had their fire and their cookpot. She said hello and watched him where he stood. The sun was already in the trees to the west and soon it would be gone all together. Only saying a few words to her in Spanish, he motioned for her to come over and to sit and eat with them.

There were two of them, a father and his teenage son and it had been the father who had invited her to share their dinner. They were eating corn tortillas heated in a pan set by the fire and in the pot simmered a kind of thick stew of meat and beans and spices that smelled of some other world she had not known existed here, but that caused her mouth to water. A bowl was fixed and tortillas given. She sat and ate as they watched her. When she had eaten one tortilla and started on the other, running it around the sides of the bowl and using it to clean the edges, the man asked his son something, then the son spoke to her in English, asking what had brought her here.

"I'm looking for my brother," she said.

The son told his father then turned and looked at her again. "Is he lost?"

"That's one way of putting it," she said. The sheep were grazing the high meadow and she looked out on them and ran her eyes across the country. She was trying to see it all before the light was gone and she marked a notch to the north where she thought she might pass through. When she brought her eyes back to the fire and the herders who sat around it, she asked how far away the Church of Eden's Gate was from where they were now sitting.

"Está buscando por la iglesia?" the father asked. His face had turned and he was watching her. "Es una mala iglesia."

Mary May looked from the father to the son and waited for the boy to translate.

"He says it is a bad place," the son said. "They have tried several times to talk with our employer. They have tried to push him, to get him to give over the sheep and to bring him around to their way of thinking."

"They have done the same to many," she said. "They are trying to do the same to me." She wiped the last of the stew up with the remaining tortilla then folded it and put it to her mouth.

"They come sometimes at night and they take a sheep. They are like wolves. They are thieves and soon, if our employer keeps losing his livestock and the money they produce, he will have no choice but to give them over for the pennies they are offering."

"The same has been done to me," she said. "They have turned

away alcohol I need for my bar in town, in Fall's End. They have cut me off from many of my distributors and scared half of them away."

"They want too much," the boy said. "They think it all belongs to them. But this land belongs to no one. It is for the people, for the sheep, it is for you to walk across and to go whichever way you please."

She looked from one to the next then thanked them for the dinner. She stood and handed back the bowl they had given her.

"A dónde vas?" the father asked.

"To get my brother," she said.

"Él está con ellos?"

"Yes," she said. She could see him thinking all this through. He stood and asked her if she would stay. He told her there was an extra blanket, that she was welcome to it. He said that it would be dark soon and he did not want her to lose her way.

He left and went back in beneath the trees again. A minute later he came out riding a big roan horse, kicking it with his heels to set it into a trot. A rifle sat beside him in an aged leather scabbard and she could see the worn wood of the buttstock. She looked after him as he went then turned to the son with the question in her eyes.

"The rifle is for the wolves, whatever form they take."

"Has it become that bad?"

"It is hard to say. It is hard to say until you are in it and you must decide. I am not sure how bad it is, but I truly cannot say. Time will tell."

"And your father?" she asked. She looked after the rider on the horse, his dark shape moving through the gray light above, the sheep moving all around him, turned away as if the horse itself were a boat breaking through the waves. "He would shoot them?"

"He will go out and give the sheep one last look before it is full dark," the son said. He had begun to clean the big pot out and to wash it with a bit of water and a cloth. "He is a herder. He has always been a herder. To take away his herd is to end his life. You understand?" He went on washing. When he looked up at Mary May again, he asked, "Your brother is a believer?"

"I don't know if he is or if he isn't," she said. "I don't know him anymore. I guess I haven't known him for a while."

"We hear things sometimes," the boy said. "We hear their chanting, or their singing. We hear voices in the woods and sometimes we see their fires. Some are believers," he said. "Others are less so. And it's these that always have it the hardest for what they think they are entering is a world defined by the mercy of God, but the place they have come is not a place of God, but a place of sinners and the word of The Father has little bearing on God, and instead The Father's words are used to enslave them."

She stood watching him and then she turned to look to where his own father was rounding the sheep in the high pasture lands above. When she turned back to the boy, she said, "You're a knowledgeable kid."

He finished with the pot then set it aside and started in on the bowls and the big ladle they had used for serving. "Just because we live out here does not mean we are blind to what is going on in town, and in all the corners of this county. Sometimes it is the distance itself, either physical or emotional, that lets you see with the most clarity."

THEY HAD STOPPED AT THE FOOT OF THE RIDGE WHEN THE DARK had come and they had eaten from the supplies Will had packed. They made a small fire and Will watched the twigs and small bits of wood fall away within the dancing heat while Lonny rolled a cigarette and told Will that he hoped tomorrow they would find her.

Will said he hoped so, too. But that he was unsure what good it would do her or do the church to bring her in. "She is not a believer," Will said. "Her family has always hated the church and I don't see how bringing her in would change that."

"It is better to have her under control than to have her loose out there," Lonny said. He lit the cigarette and sat smoking. "She was talking to the sheriff before all this."

"What was she saying to him?"

"Nothing of any truth," Lonny said. "But she is casting doubt upon The Father and upon the church and I think that alone is something John cannot stand about her."

"I knew her as a kid," Will said. "She was strong-willed even then. I don't expect she's changed much since."

"We will see," Lonny said. He smoked the cigarette and looked in on the flames, then when he was done he flicked the cigarette away into the fire. Five minutes later he was asleep.

Will watched the fire until it was only an incandescent flicker of coal there at the bottom of the pit he had constructed from loose stones he'd found nearby. He thought of the bear cub and how he had wanted to save it, but that in the end he had not been able to.

That night for the first time in a long time he dreamt of his daughter. She had always liked him to sit up by her bed and she would not go to sleep unless he was there next to her. When she had been young she would wake up screaming if she found the chair empty and him not there. Will dreamt of her there in bed with her eyes closed but her mind still wide awake.

"You won't leave me?" she said.

"No. I'm going to sit right here."

"Even when I fall asleep you'll be right there?"

"Yes," he said. "I'm going to be right here. I'm going to be look-ing over you and I'll never leave you."

"What about Mamma?" she asked.

"What about her?"

"Who is looking over her?"

"I am. I am watching over both of you."

"Even while you're watching over me?"

"Yes," he said. He observed her for a while. He listened to her breathing. He heard the way her breath changed as she went to sleep. He was sitting in the old room that had been hers, sitting in the house that had been his and his wife's and that had sat up above on the bluff. And in the dream, he could see out on the landscape through the bedroom window and there was a golden and full char-acter to the land that seemed to him like the dry wheat of a field seen just before the harvest.

He got up from the chair and went out of the room and closed the door. He stopped for a moment, knowing his daughter was in there and that she was safe and that she was alive. Now he went and looked for his wife, but he could not find her. He stood in the kitchen and looked out on the same field. It was dark now, nothing to see but his own reflection in the glass and it seemed to him that the house had changed and that much was missing in the reflected glass of the world behind him.

When he turned from the window he heard his daughter's pierc-ing scream, calling for him, calling for him to come and get her like he had done when she was a little girl and she would wake up startled to find herself alone.

He was at her door as if he had simply found it waiting there but each time he turned the knob it would not unlock and he could hear her screaming for him, asking where he was, asking for him to come and find her. He kept turning the knob in his hand and it was doing nothing and he knew without a doubt that something horrible was happening that he could not stop, that even in his home there was nothing he could do to help her.

He woke with a start, and he could not stop coughing. It was still an hour before the dawn would come, but he could see the light building in the east. He held a hand to his mouth and racked his lungs and felt something stir within him and come loose. He spit it from his mouth and sat staring at it. Mucus, dark and evil looking there on the ground like some Precambrian life form brought forth from within the mud.

After an hour he was still awake, just lying there watching above as the sun chased the last remaining stars from out of the sky. On the ground beside him, dark as a pool of tar was the blackened and drying blood of an ulcer or some other wickedness he had brought up from somewhere deep inside.

THE BOY WOKE HER IN THE MORNING WITH A HAND HELD OUT across her shoulder and as she opened her eyes he backed away toward the fire and he sat again and stirred whatever it was he had been making there in the pot. His father sat beside him, both of them there like they had never left, still wearing the same clothes and sitting in the same place.

"Estabas hablando," the father said.

She shook her head to show she did not understand then looked toward the boy and waited.

"You were talking in your sleep," the boy said. Using the ladle, he scooped dark liquid from within the pot then put it in a bowl and handed it to her. He was back at the fire again when she looked up. She sniffed the bowl, blew on it then put the liquid to her lips and tasted it. "Coffee?" she said. "Gracias."

"De nada," the father said. The boy nodded, dipping the ladle again and serving his father before he served himself.

When she was finished with the bowl she could see the loose grinds at the bottom and she thought about the cowboy stories the old ones who came into the bar used to tell about reading the grinds to tell the future. And though she stared down for a minute or more she could not tell a thing from what she saw. She rose, tipping the bowl over and using her fingers to clean out the grinds.

The bruise was still there on her thigh when she squatted down within the trees. She ran her hand across it, pressing against it to feel the tenderness of the skin. It was purple, going blue to yellow at the edges, and when she was done she lifted her pants and came out from under the trees buttoning up her jeans.

The boy had saddled up the horse and he was waiting for her. "You'll go to find your brother now?"

"I'm going to try."

The boy offered her his hand. "I can give you a ride as far as the high ridge," he said. "The church is beyond another few miles and you may be able to see the smoke but I still think it is a bad idea."

She looked at him then took his hand and pulled herself up behind him. The father came forward now. He held the chrome .38 in the flat palm of his hand like some offering.

"It was in your bedding," the boy said, looking down at the gun in his father's hand.

She looked at the father then looked to the boy. She thanked him and took the revolver. "It was my father's," she said, then, realizing she knew the word in Spanish, she said to him, "De mi padre."

"Dónde está tu padre?"

"Dead. A car accident."

The father clucked his tongue and shook his head. He offered his condolences. The boy started the horse up across the field, Mary May with her hands about the waist of the boy as they went, and the sheep parting around them like whitecaps seen in an ocean storm.

When she looked back toward the small campground she could only see the rise of smoke, dying now as somewhere down there the boy's father prepared for another day.

The boy climbed the ridge, moving the horse one way and then another on a path that Mary May could see had been used before. When they came to the top the boy slid down and helped her from the horse. He pointed out the valley below and showed her where the church was, down across the valley over a few hills and farther on to where the lake lay.

"Your brother is all you have, isn't he?"

"Yes," she said.

WILL LOST THE TRAIL COMING UP THE AVALANCHE CHUTE. Several times he had to backtrack and find it before he could go on only to lose it again. When they came out on top of the ridge he could see it would be no help. The windswept rock barren of any sign.

He walked the edge of the ridge and looked down over the precipice at the rocks below, broad fans of talus and broken rock spread across the slope into the river valley farther on. It disappeared among the sedge, and then farther on he saw the thick darkness again of trees and brush.

When he came back, walking along the ridge the opposite way, he could see the white backs of the sheep moving in the mountain field opposite from where he stood. They were high on the mountain and he watched a rider move through them, seeing how the sheep began to part to let the rider through.

"That's where I'd go," Will said. "Cold and lost. I'd go to where the people are." He looked to where Lonny was standing. He pointed out the rider and the sheep. He took up his rifle and passed the scope across the field then handed the rifle over to Lonny. "I count two men," Will said. "I don't see Mary May."

Lonny took a long look through the scope then handed it back to Will. "That's where you'd go?"

"That's where I'd go," Will said.

By midmorning they had crossed the river and climbed up the mountain into the field. The sheep moved about them as they walked and the two herders now stood to watch them come.

"Buenos días," the older of the two said. He had come forward a bit from the dead firepit and watched them as they walked closer.

Will raised a hand and returned the greeting, afterward turning to look back over his shoulder at Lonny. "You speak any Spanish?"

Lonny shook his head. He was watching the two herders and he looked to Will now. "The only Mexicans I ever knew were in prison and they might as well have been in another country the way the place was divided up."

Will looked back toward the man. "You speak any English?"

The man looked backwards at the boy, who Will could now see must have been the man's son. The son just stood there looking at the two of them and he shook his head.

"Estamos buscando . . ." Will said. He was trying to think up what to say, but he didn't know the words. He had worked a few summers in the fields to the east when he had come back from the war, but it was a long time ago and even then he had not spoken much Spanish. "Estamos buscando for someone," he said, making a wide and somewhat futile gesture of the surrounding world.

Again, the father looked toward the boy. The boy shrugged.

"These guys don't know what the fuck you're talking about," Lonny said. He went to stand at the fire and looked down upon the blackened rocks. "Ask them if they have any fucking food? Or liquor?" he said, looking over at Will, not even bothering to ask the father or the son. "I'd kill one of these sheep if it meant we had something to bring back out of here for John and the rest at the church."

"Iglesia?" the father asked. He raised a hand to his chin and pantomimed stroking the long beards both Will and Lonny wore, along with all the rest of the men of Eden's Gate.

"Yes," Will said. "Iglesia. Both of us." He pointed to Lonny then brought his hand back and put it to his chest. "Iglesia."

"Ask them about the food," Lonny said again. He had begun to walk around the small camp and he was toeing at the supplies there and the various camp ware. The boy was watching him. "Hell, ask them if they have any liquor? Maybe we'll get lucky."

Will raised a hand to his mouth. "Comida?" he asked. He was speaking to the father, but he brought his eyes around on the son.

"No," the father said.

"No?" Lonny said. "Tell them they're being rude." He spoke to Will but he looked now to the boy who was standing a few feet off. "You're being fucking rude," Lonny said. "You understand you motherfucking mute?" Lonny leaned down, looked in under the trees then started to walk away toward where a horse was tethered. "I'm going to take their horse and take their sheep and ride the fuck out of here. I'm done with whatever this is we're doing."

The boy came around and stood between Lonny and the horse.

In his hand was a small knife that he was holding about waist-high in front of him.

Lonny raised his hands then turned and looked toward Will and to the father. A small half smile began to spread across his face. Will didn't even see what happened next, it seemed that fast. The boy was on the ground with blood streaming from his nostrils, Lonny standing over him, one of his boots already across the wrist that held the knife.

The father turned but Will was close and he broadsided the man and sent him to the ground. Will took the rifle from his shoulder and held it on the man just as he tried to get back to his feet. The sound of Will moving the bolt forward froze the man in place.

The boy tried to bring his other hand across and take the knife but Lonny bent and punched him hard in the ribs then reached and twisted the knife away. He stood and tossed the knife and backed away a little as the boy wheezed and tried to gather his breath.

"Stop," Will said, watching all of this, watching Lonny where he stood and watching the boy. "He was only trying to protect what's his."

"What's his?" Lonny asked, his voice elevated in a tone of disbelief. "What's his?" He took a step away from the boy then he turned and pivoted and brought his boot up fast and kicked the boy so hard he left the ground. The boy was wheezing and rolling on the ground, trying to get his hands and knees beneath him.

"Stop it," Will said again. He could see the same wild smile come across Lonny's face.

Lonny kicked the boy twice in the side as the boy tried to get to his feet and he was rolling now away from Lonny and Lonny was going after him, kicking him time after time. Huffing with the effort. "When are they going to learn? When are they all going to fucking learn their lesson?" he was saying. "What's theirs is mine. They think they know better than me or John. They think they can just close their eyes and look away." He kicked the boy again. He bent and grabbed the boy at his shirt collar and brought him up and he started punching him now, raising the boy toward him with one hand on his collar and punching him with the other.

Will was on Lonny almost as soon as he'd made up his mind he had to stop it. He dragged Lonny backwards, the rifle underneath Lonny's chin and Will backing, one hand on the stock and the other on the barrel, choking Lonny and dragging him from the campground. "You were going to kill him," Will said. "Calm down. Calm the fuck down."

The father had risen and he had bent over his son and Will could see the son's slow movements and see that he had been beaten badly but that he was still alive and still conscious. Will dragged Lonny farther and he could feel Lonny start to slacken. He eased the rifle off his throat and asked him if he would calm the fuck down.

When Will let him go, Lonny stood there rubbing at his throat. He looked toward the camp where the father still knelt, trying to help his son. "There's no one here," Lonny said.

"That doesn't mean you can kill them."

"You saw how they reacted when I talked about the church."

"I saw how they reacted when you threatened to steal from them. You need to calm down, Lonny. You need to think."

He was still rubbing at his throat, and he looked to Will. "It's time they knew. It's time they all knew what is coming for them."

"What's that?" Will said.

"The end is coming and they can help us and be saved or they can go against us and burn with all the rest."

Will watched Lonny. He didn't know what to say. "You're a fucking lunatic," Will finally got out.

"No," Lonny said. "I'm a survivor. And all of us are riding in the ark and some of us just don't know it yet."

Will looked to Lonny and then he looked to where the father knelt trying to comfort his son. When Will approached, the father turned and held an upraised palm toward Will and said, "Ella fue a la iglesia. Allá." He moved his hand, pointing past Will to the ridge above.

Will turned and looked. He thought about saying something more, but there was nothing more to say that would make it any better. Something was going on here that he did not understand and he looked to Lonny and then looked up at the ridge.

THE HAWK PASSED AGAIN, THE SHADOW NOW SHOWING IN THE grass as the bird turned, rising on the thermals. Mary May was halfway across the broad field that ran the bottom of the valley and she turned now to look upward on the sky, trying to see where the hawk had gone.

Though she had known in some way that what she was attempting was beyond any real sense or hope, she had gone ahead anyway. Now she was walking in the direction the boy had shown her, working over and over in her mind the question he had asked.

"Your brother is all you have?"

Drew was three years younger than her and he had been the last, along with the rest of his class, to graduate from the high school before they shut it down. There was a time afterwards where she had just worked. She had worked the bar and she had done her thing as she had always done and she had not thought about him but to share a meal from time to time, or see him in passing at their parents' place. She had kept her head down and she had saved and tried to help her parents with the bar.

When he came in and told her that he had joined the army and would soon be leaving, she had not known what to say. She realized for a long time, ever since they had been kids together, she had never talked to him, she had never truly thought to ask him anything of any real depth.

She walked on. She thought about what the herder boy had asked her next. She thought about what he'd said to her, he had wondered what she would do when she found him. He had wondered what would happen if she found her brother to be someone other than who she thought he was.

"I hope you mean the same to him as he means to you," the boy had said. He had turned the horse around right there and with a little nod to her he was gone down the ridge the way he'd come.

WILL CAME UP THE RIDGE WITH LONNY FOLLOWING. THEY USED the switchback path that showed the horse tracks in the dirt. But that was mostly covered with sedge and the droppings of many sheep.

When Will looked back down the sheep were still there in the field but he could see nothing of the camp that was beneath the trees. He had said little to Lonny since they'd left, but he could hear Lonny grumbling over it from time to time and complaining that they should have at least taken the horse if they meant to catch up to Mary May.

"Is that how it is?" Will asked. "Us versus them?"

"That's how it's always been," Lonny said.

"When they came to me and offered me a place with them I was grateful for it. They did not force my hand."

"Simpler times," Lonny said. "The time is coming when it won't be that simple anymore and the more we have among us—the more we have that are willing to hear The Father's words—the better all of us will be."

"You act like the end of the world will come tomorrow."

"It might not come tomorrow, or the next day, but that doesn't mean it is not coming. People like you and me will survive."

"What kind of people are we?" Will asked.

"We're people who do what they need to do."

"Not if it means pushing other people under," Will said.

"You and me," Lonny said. "We see the world in different ways, but we are no different."

"We all have our purpose," Will said, playing off what Lonny had told him at the empty Kershaw farm.

"That's right," Lonny said. "That's what John says all the time. We all have our purpose. We all must do our duty for the church."

They came to the top of the ridge and Will could see it was much like the other they had moved over earlier that morning. One side a gradual slope, while the other, the side that they now came to, fell away almost as if it had been scooped from the rock by the hand of some celestial being. Steep and perilous and littered below with rock and talus that had fallen from the very spot they now were standing.

Will stopped and looked down at the valley below. He waited for Lonny to take the last few steps and then when the man came up and stood beside him, Will took the rifle from his shoulder, flipped the lens cover up on the scope, and put the lens to his eye. There was a wide valley below with a broad field of sedge and Junegrass and he ran his vision upon it. When he brought his eye away he almost could not believe that he had found Mary May.

She was walking down the middle of the field and he could see that she would be into the far wood in the next quarter mile. He placed the scope to his eye again and marked her. When he brought the scope away again, he looked down into the field. She was a tiny thing there in the depths and he knew that with the naked eye he would have missed her.

Without taking his eyes away, he handed the rifle over to Lonny. "Take a look," Will said. He was watching the tiny figure out there below them. A hawk was circling high above and it was a speck itself, riding on the thermals. "You see the hawk out there? Put the scope on it and then run the lens down all the way to the meadow."

He watched Lonny now. He watched Lonny find the hawk and then he watched Lonny move the scope down and find Mary May.

"John will be very happy," Lonny said. He brought his eye away from the scope and looked to Will and in that same moment a rifle fired that was not the one Lonny held in his two hands.

Will turned and moved toward the sound. It was down in the mountain field out of which they had just climbed. The rifle fired again and he heard the echo of the shot and the reverberation as the sound spread from one side of the valley to the other. Then Will started to hear more shots, automatic gunfire, and the big booming of a shotgun.

At first he had thought maybe the herder and his son had followed them. Or had taken up some position to better take revenge. But now as Will peered back over a loose conglomeration of rocks on the sheep and the meadow below, he could see the herder had started shooting at five men now moving up across the meadow—moving exactly toward where Will and Lonny now had come.

Out front and leading the men, amid the surging sheep that

swirled and stampeded in a sort of whirling sweep of white, was John Seed. He held in front of him a large metal antenna shaped almost like a wire grid. Will knew it immediately and he knew that John was not hunting wolves, but that he was hunting them and hunting Mary May and Will should have known it from the start.

The herder fired again and John's men ducked and then rose, shooting over the backs of the sheep as they came up through the field. Will watched one man, holding an AK-47, strafe the campsite, the bullets raking across the dirt.

Several more single rifle shots were fired from the sheep camp but Will could not see the herders. They were somewhere beneath the trees and they were firing on the men as they moved in among the sheep. A moment later he heard the clop of the hooves and he saw the two herders doubled on the horse, riding fast along the bottom of the meadow and away. Several of John's men were shooting at them, taking shots as they rose and fired again over the backs of sheep.

Will might not have heard the click of his rifle had they kept on shooting. But as close to him, and as familiar to him as it was, he turned almost in the same instant Lonny pushed the safety forward on the rifle. Lonny's eye was to the scope and the barrel faced down toward the valley in which Mary May was walking, and Lonny did not need to push the .308 cartridge forward with the bolt, because Will now realized with horror that he had already done it for him.

MARY MAY WAS THREE QUARTERS OF THE WAY ACROSS THE meadow when she heard the thunder. She stopped and looked toward the sky. Blue as a robin's egg. She turned and looked toward the ridge she had descended from and she took a few steps back the way she'd come.

She heard the pulse of thunder again, but she knew it was not thunder. The booming sound was diffuse and more of a rumble, just as distant thunder might sometimes be. But around it, and at the edge of this new sound, was the snap of gunfire that she knew well enough and that she had heard all through her life out here in the country.

She was looking up toward the ridge and she was wondering whether whatever had happened could be helped and she moved now, walking with purpose back the way she'd come. Soon she was running and she had taken out the .38. She held it tight in her hand to make sure she would not lose it. She came nearly halfway across the field when the firing stopped and there was a strange moment when the world returned to normal. Just a breeze working across the meadow, and the sun above, and the far branches of trees wavering a little in the wind.

The rifle shot that passed her was no more than a foot from her, traveling in the air then thudding into the ground another ten feet on. She felt the air move, she turned and saw where the dust had bloomed up from off the ground and then as she stood there, beginning to realize what was happening, she heard the distant shot of the rifle sound from right there atop the ridge.

WILL MADE IT TO LONNY JUST AS HE PULLED THE TRIGGER. WILL bowled him over and sent him to his back. The rifle came loose from his hands and Will watched it skitter atop rock for a moment then fall over the edge of the ridge and disappear.

Lonny came up off the ground with his hands out on either side of him like a wrestler taking up his stance.

"You were going to shoot her," Will said. They stood no more than five feet apart and Will watched Lonny circle downslope, his hands still out, his eyes never leaving Will.

"Better to do it here than to do it somewhere else. Better if it seems like she went into the woods and never came back out."

"Christ, Lonny. We were told to find her. We were told to find her and help her out."

Lonny struck out fast with a single fist and Will only had time to fall away and catch himself with one hand. He scrambled back to his feet, feeling too old and too slow to be any match for the quickness Lonny brought with each movement. Lonny was smiling at him and he whipped out a fist again that brushed past Will's right cheek. Both still wore their packs and it made their movements awkward and a little counterweighted as Will circled the edge of the ridge then came down, trying to stay just out of Lonny's reach.

"Pretty limber for an old guy," Lonny said. He came inside and popped one fist up hard, catching Will in the ribs. "But still an old guy." Will bent double, dry heaving. Lonny brought the opposite fist down hard against his cheekbone.

Will fell facedown against the smooth windswept rock of the ridge. His face was on fire from where Lonny had knocked him and his belly muscles were cramping and pulling on each other like some tug of war within his stomach. He tried to roll but Lonny kicked him and Will—using the force of the kick to move downslope—fell off a ledge of rock and landed another four feet down.

He felt like someone had thrown dynamite at his feet and he had been launched upward only to land, barely whole, forty feet away. He wasn't sure if anything was broken and pieces of him ached and hurt like they had not hurt for years, but he knew he needed to get up. He knew he needed to help himself, and he knew he needed to stop Lonny from whatever it was he was doing.

Will stood fast, just as Lonny came to the edge of the small ledge. He took one of Lonny's feet and pulled back hard. Will heard bone hitting the rock as Lonny landed first on his backpack, then the residual force whipped his head down and his skull bounced then resettled against the top of the ledge. Now Will moved around, wheezing with one hand held atop his belly. He came around the ledge while Lonny was still gathering himself together, now turning on his side. There was blood in his hair and on the rock where his skull had hit.

Before Will could get to him Lonny had risen to one knee. He pushed himself fully upright and Will circled, looking for anything that he might use to defend himself with. Lonny brought his fists up again and came at him. There were loose rocks nearby that Will thought to reach for, but grabbing for them would put him again within Lonny's reach.

Will backed as far as he could. He was moving toward the edge now and Lonny moved after him. Blood was wet against the side of Lonny's neck where it had fallen from his hairline. Will looked again behind him but he could see nothing to stop himself from going over. The rifle was down there somewhere. Ten feet? Fifty? A hundred feet below? He turned again, inches from the edge. He could see the rifle now. It had landed on a small outcropping, three feet down. Will began to move but in that instant, just as he decided this might be his only chance, Lonny swung, his right hand striking out as Will tried to duck and move for the rifle just below.

The fist would have struck him if he hadn't decided just a half second before to go for the rifle. But as it happened, with Lonny already off balance, already woozy and bleeding from the back of his head, he went over. Will turned just as the fist passed by him, followed by Lonny's twisting body, arm outstretched as his forward momentum carried him across the edge of the ridge and out into the broad space beyond.

Will saw him falling. It seemed like a minute before Lonny hit, but it must have been merely a second or two. The body landed in the loose rock and talus a hundred feet below then bounced awkwardly as it somersaulted and careened, legs and arms stretched outward down the slope, sliding to a stop amid the larger boulders toward the bottom of the cliff debris.

Will stood there staring down. One of Lonny's arms lay behind him in strange backwards rapture, while his face looked upward and his head appeared like it had been popped and then stretched away from off his body. The skin of the neck the only thing to keep it now attached.

Will bent and lay against the edge of the ridge. He reached a hand for the rifle and came up holding it by the stock. Quickly he worked the bolt and checked the rifle over, moving it to one side then the other in a quick study of wood and metal. It seemed okay but there was a crack in the lens when he raised his eye to it and looked again down into the empty meadow he had seen Mary May passing across only minutes before.

AS HER LUNGS BEAT, PULLING AT THE AIR LIKE THE AIR ITSELF was not enough and the capillaries in her heart burst like distant stars, far away but looming ever closer—she ran. Flat out, full speed ahead, no looking back, no pause, no fucking way she was letting anyone catch her. In the checkered light of shadow and sun that came streaming down through the pines, the world bounced across her vision with the frenetic pull of some devil's hacksaw, raking away at the earth from down below.

It was only the sheer terror and realization that each footfall and beat of her sole could be heard against rock and pine needle that caused her to pull up short. She veered to her right and stood stock-still, with her back to the thin trunk of a tall pine, trying as best she could to catch her breath. She was immediately aware of how alone she was, how very lost she was from any comfort or salvation. Out there in the wider brightness of the field from which she ran, she could see no one and she had heard nothing since the bullet flew past her and struck the ground no more than ten feet off.

She needed to get away and she needed to get away now. She looked around at the half-lit forest. She knew now why so many of the original pioneers were lost in places like this. The lodgepole pines everywhere she looked, straight as arrows, thick as telephone poles, each the same, like the makings of some carnival funhouse there was no escaping from.

WILL CAME DOWN OFF THE RIDGE, HALF SLIDING AND HALF walking through the loose gravel that lined the bottom of the cliff. When he came to Lonny, the man's eyes were still and open and a savage gash could be seen across the side of his head that ran all the way along one cheek and up across the skin just above his ear. His neck was clearly broken and the skin had bruised and even as Will took hold of an arm, meaning to turn him over, Will could feel the lifelessness of his body and the looseness of the muscle.

Will rolled and pushed Lonny over. He was lighter than Will but he was by no means easy to move, and as Will pushed he could

smell already the turning of the body and the release of all its liq-
uids. He pushed Lonny all the way over and now he could get his
hands on Lonny's pack.

Undoing the drawstring at the top he began to pull item after
item from the backpack and lay them out. Much of it Will had seen
already when they'd made their camp the night before. But when
he came to the wolf collar with the transmitter he was not at all
surprised. He pulled it up and stood looking at it. He turned it over
in his hand. It weighed little more than a few pounds and he could
see where there was a little switch that could be turned on and then
turned off.

For ten seconds, he stood there looking at it, then he slid the collar back inside the bag with all the rest of Lonny's things and pulled
the man over and let him rest. Up above Will could see the place he
had once stood and he looked now into the field another hundred
or so feet down slope. He set off in the direction he had seen Mary
May heading, knowing that Eden's Gate was not far off.

When he had made it all the way across the field he could see
figures moving on the ridge. He watched them where they formed
just at the lip of the cliff. Will moved under the trees now, not wanting to be seen. Once he was in the shade he raised the scope and
put his eye on them, watching as they looked down on the place
Will knew Lonny to be.

Will watched them long enough to see them break apart from
their small group and move out along the ridge in single file. He
watched them come to the place that Will himself had found to
thread his way down from atop the cliff. And then Will watched
them move across the loose rock and talus just as he had done.
John walked out front, leading with the antenna, no doubt moving
toward the transponder and the wolf collar within Lonny's bag.

• • •

MARY MAY HAD WAITED JUST LONG ENOUGH TO SEE HOW MANY had been following her. She watched the distant shape of a single man move down and away from the far ridge as he cut through the grass almost in the same path that she had surely followed. She could see the rifle on his back and she watched him stop midway through, studying something he saw there in the grass.

Without giving any more time for the man to catch her, she removed her boots and stuffed her socks down within. Then, with boots in hand and the .38 stuck back down the waist of her pants she set out, moving fast and making her way up a small rise to the north she knew might give her a vantage of the land. She was careful with her movements as she went, knowing the man had tracked her this far and could likely track her farther.

She moved barefoot over the forest bed of pine needles and she stopped often to look back at her trail. She was leaving less of one but she could still see in places the scuff of one foot followed by the other. She had grown up in these woods. She had been trained by her father and his friends to track and hunt and she knew an experienced hunter could track just about anything over almost anything, except the smoothest rock or water.

With hands outstretched she moved onward up the slope as she made her way to the slight rise above. The slope now growing ever steeper in a way she had not calculated for, much of it hidden behind the dense trunks and underbrush of the forest. Halfway up she fell and slid four feet down and getting to her feet she saw the dark scrape she had made there in the pine needles. She could do nothing for it and she moved now, quicker even than she had gone before.

Soon she gained the rise and with a single scanning look down the way she'd come, she drew herself up and over a large outcropping of rock there. Laying herself out flat so that she could present the smallest profile. The rock on which she lay was like some backbone across the topmost portion of the rise, but unlike the ridges and ranges she had crossed through earlier it did not offer the view she had been hoping for. The rise only high enough above the forest floor to offer up the briefest view of the land beyond.

In the silence that followed, as she listened to her heart beating in her chest, she thought she heard the sound of breathing. She held her own breath, steadying herself where she hid. In the far distance, she heard the call of a shrike dusted up from somewhere on the other side of the rise. The bird's anxious call settling in across the forest as it flapped up along the rise then came out above, moving past and then away, threading its way down into the trees beyond.

For only a second did she keep her eyes on the path of this bird. She knew maybe it had simply startled up out of some tree, called from the branches by some prey or thing it hunted. But she also knew this was only hopeful thinking, that somewhere down below there was a man tracking her with a rifle.

For a beat, she looked down into the gray muted light of the forest. Afternoon was settling in and the sun had begun to move away beneath the trees. She pulled herself back, moving on her stomach until she could stand safely out of view. Somewhere down below she knew she would come to a road and farther on the church, and hopefully if she could find him, her brother.

She had grown up in the county and she knew these roads, she knew the forests and the mountains. And though she had never gone this far into the woods, or off the paths that lined and connected many of the lakes and mountains in the area, she knew where the county road ran the edge of the Eden's Gate property and she charted a course in her head to get there. Pines and aspen on the slope then paper birch below that ran out and moved across boggy lowlands a mile on. She'd have cover all the way down the slope into the lowlands before she started coming across sedge and grassland right before the road.

She took one last look over the edge of the rock outcropping before she turned and moved downslope. A couple hundred feet on she came to a dead stop and looked back up toward where she'd been. In the exact spot she had picked to lay upon her belly, was a man seen standing at the top of the rise there looking down on her.

WILL DID NOT PUT THE RIFLE ON HER OR EVEN MAKE A SINGLE movement. He stood atop the small rise and looked down toward her. She had grown up considerably since he'd seen her last. She wore jeans and a T-shirt and a dirty, zippered sweatshirt. She carried her boots in her hands. She stood there looking back at him and if she recognized him at all she did not show it.

She was off and running before he could say a thing and for only a second he let her go. He knew where she was going and though she had removed her boots and changed her track, he could see now that he would have little trouble following her. What did concern him was the ache and sickness he had started to feel at his core. He was moving now slightly bent over with a hand across his belly where Lonny had connected with a fist and then delivered kick after kick. Will knew whatever damage had been done, a bruised organ or a cracked rib, the adrenaline of his fight with Lonny had hidden it. And now as he went on that feeling was wearing off and each step seemed to pain him further.

He watched the place she had been standing, then he set off

down the rise and came into the wood. For a moment, he could see her running, the light coming through the pines above flashing on her as she moved. He took several steps forward, the ache and pain in his stomach now showing on his face. He stopped and looked to where he had seen her last, but she was not there. He wondered how much time he had. He wondered about Lonny and what Lonny had said to him before Will had moved and watched the man go over.

Then, standing there, he bent double and the insides of his stomach came up and splattered across the ground. He went down on a knee and the relief he felt was almost immediate. He could breathe again and the muscles of his stomach had come free from the knot that had bound them up so tight. Will could see blood in the vomit and he wondered again what evil thing might reside within him, whether it was an ulcer, or whether it was simply Lonny beating the shit out of him only a half hour before. But there was no time to dwell on it as he rose to his feet again then looked back the way he'd come.

John and four of his men were still out there and if any of them were trackers they would come upon him soon. Will looked back upon the rise and the path he'd taken down from it. He was unsure what to do. He was unsure what would happen, or what had been meant to happen all this time.

John had said he wanted to help Mary May, as John and The Father had once helped Will so long ago.

Will turned and looked again to where he had last seen her. He'd lost too much time and he knew it. She was scared and now she knew she was being followed. He called her name low at first and then stepping forward he cupped his two hands to his mouth and yelled her name. He had said he would protect her. He had said he would keep her safe and he would help her, but he could not do that if she ran. He could do nothing for her if he could not catch her. He called her name again. "Mary May," he called. He let the name linger in the air and then he yelled again.

MARY MAY TURNED AND LOOKED BACK THE WAY SHE'D COME AS soon as she heard her name. She hesitated and for a second she thought about stopping. But there had been no denying the fact that she had been shot at, that the man who had likely shot at her was out there following her still, and that like a hunter using an elk call, this man was hunting her, calling out her name, hoping that it would stop her and draw her near.

Twenty minutes later Mary May saw the road. She had back-tracked and crosscut the forest behind her in such a fashion that future archeologists looking over the casts of her movements in the mud would wonder if she were not already wounded in some way, delirious, and headed straight for whatever tar pit might be close at hand.

She came out of the trees into patches of dogwood and mountain ash, dotted here and there with clearings of sedge. Her legs burned slightly and her hands and forearms, though tough from years of working the bar, were scratched and dappled with minor cuts and bruises.

She had no idea where the man who hunted her had gone, and she had seen no more of him. She stopped and just listened to the forest, then satisfied he was gone she put her boots back on one at a time. A mile or so up and over the ridge was the sound of a big truck running down through its gears as it came out of the northern mountains. She tried to listen for more but all she fathomed from it was that perhaps it was a logging truck, though that seemed false to her, the church already having bought and closed the mill years before.

When she reached the road, she did not go directly out. The light was fading and she was beginning to feel the cold. She had no way of knowing exactly where Eden's Gate was, whether it was right or left, but she was certain it was on this road. She was shivering slightly, the dusk was settling in and the thought of spending another night out here was beginning to weigh heavily on her mind. She stepped now onto the road and she began to run, feeling her lungs beat inside her chest and the air move across her skin.

When the headlights broke from around a bend in the road far off and spread their light toward her she was quick to drop off the road and hide herself within the underbrush. But the vehicle did not pass her by. It stopped fifty feet away, its headlights reaching out across the pavement, and the dusky light of the setting sun giving everything a tinge of auburn red.

She heard a door open, then she heard the sound of boots on cement and she watched the shape of a man walk out and through the light of the headlights as he came toward her. She backed now, increasing her distance, almost certain she would run. Almost certain she would need to dive headlong through the brush, that whoever had seen her would go after her and finish whatever had been started days before.

But when she heard her name it was not the same voice she had heard calling to her in the mountains. It was not John's voice or any she had heard in a very long time. She stood now and she came forward. She heard her name called again. She walked up onto the road, almost disbelieving she had found him, or that it was him that had actually found her.

"Drew?" she said.

He stood looking down on her from there atop the road. He was thinner than she remembered, but bigger in the chest and in the shoulders and though he was bearded, his skin and eyes were much the same and she knew he was the same brother she had so often thought about and that her father had gone to find.

"Drew," she said again, just to say it, just to speak his name as if she feared she might not get another chance.

"It's me," he said. He walked forward and put a hand out and he pulled her up from out of the roadside ditch. He was a few inches taller than her and he pulled her into him and hugged her, holding her for a long time.

"You heard about Daddy?" she asked. "And Mamma?"

He let her go. He stood close to her, his arms still holding her shoulders. "I heard," he said. "I heard what happened."

"He tried to come and get you." The tears were coming now and she could not stop them. She looked away and he pulled her close again and she could feel the way he held her. She could feel the way his lungs moved and she let her head down onto his chest and she cried for what seemed a very long while.

When she was done, when she had pulled away and had wiped a hand across her eyes, he said, "Let's get you home. Let's get you somewhere warm. Let's get you some food and water. Let's get you somewhere safe."

She looked at him for a time and she stood there waiting and thinking of what to say next. She could hardly believe he was here, that he had found her and that he would take her away from this and everything could be the way it had always been meant to be.

"Come on," he said.

He started to lead her back to the truck, but she stopped and then he stopped. She was looking at the insignia on the side of the truck and then she was looking up at him. "The truck? You're driving one of their trucks. One of their church trucks."

He looked at her like she might be crazy. He ran his eyes from her to the truck then back again. "You're going to be okay," he said. "You're going to be just fine. I'm going to take you home. You'll see. I'm your brother. You're going to be fine with me."

She looked at him. She let what he had said sit between them. "You'll take me home?" she asked. "And you'll come with me?"

"Yes," he said. "Now get in the truck and let me help you."

WILL CAME TO THE ROAD JUST AS THE BRAKE LIGHTS FLARED ON and the truck moved away. He watched the taillights until they were gone from sight. He had seen the road from higher up and he had seen the truck stop, then Mary May come up out of the ditch with the man standing over her, offering her his hand.

Almost in the same instant Will had gone crashing down through the dogwood and ash that had started to populate the land. He came out into the clearing before the road, knelt and swung the rifle around and looked through the scope to where the truck had parked there in the middle of the lane. Mary May was holding onto the man and Will put the crosshairs on him and waited for the man to release her. When he had—when he had stepped back from her and turned toward the truck—Will could see him now clear as he had seen Mary May standing there on the mountain looking back at him. It was her brother, Drew. Will let the rifle down and, with one knee still down in the dirt of the field just before the road, he watched both siblings climb into the truck and drive away.

Now, he walked the road for fifty feet and then stood looking out down the empty pavement. The light was all but gone, the blue of night settling in, and he could hear the chirping of frogs in the ditch off the side of the road. When he turned and looked opposite he found a lone maple tree standing in the middle of a clearing. And though it was not yet late summer, the leaves had turned and many had begun to fall and litter the ground below.

Will came down off the road, took a wide step across the ditch, and walked out into the field. The ground was boggy and in places he could see a foul mud that held atop it a greasy oil. He walked almost to the tree, but stopped just before it and stood looking up into the branches, knowing for its height and width that it had lived a long time in this place and might have lived even longer had the earth itself not changed.

As he stood there he could see several leaves come loose then drift down. The tree was not barren but it likely would be soon.

When John's voice called to him from behind, Will did not turn. He kept looking up at the tree and wondering just how long it would go on.

"You did good," John said. "Mary May is with us now. You helped to save her."

Will turned. John stood there looking at him. Farther on, back by the road his men were standing, all of them with their weapons held crossways in their arms. Tired looking but at rest. "And Lonny?" Will asked. "He said he meant to kill her."

"Yes," John said. "I saw how he was going. I should have seen it sooner."

"Sooner?"

"His drinking. The loosening of his faith. He was not a true believer," John said. "He was breaking away from us, breaking away and falling in among his own past sins."

"That's why you tracked us? That's why you followed us up the mountain?"

"Yes," John said. "I could not trust him. I did not know if I could trust you. Lonny used to say you were an enigma."

A leaf fell again, and it fluttered and flipped, end over end, then came to rest between them. "Enigma?"

"It was not the word he used," John said. "But I see now that he was the one that could not be trusted. I should have seen it earlier. I should have known all of it, all he said and all he did, was all leading up to this."

"I did not mean to kill him."

"You didn't kill him," John said. "You would have never done a thing like that. He simply fell. He toppled over a cliff and he fell and broke his neck. It was an accident and all of us could see that clearly. His blood is not on your hands."

Will locked eyes with John as he put a hand to Will's shoulder.

"You are still with us. You are part of who we are. You have provided us with a service and we are thankful for you and all you do. There is no shame in this. Once you had owed us everything, but that time has long passed and it is us who now owe you. We will take you back to Eden's Gate and there you will receive your blessing and we will give you a place to rest and help you just as you have helped us. You are still with us, aren't you, Will?"

"Of course," Will said, not knowing what else he could say.

"We have given you salvation. But you too have given us your soul."

"Yes," Will said. "I know that. I never stopped knowing that."

"Good," John said. "The Father will be glad to hear it. He waits for you. He waits to give you his blessing once again. You will stay at Eden's Gate tonight and you will be my guest and The Father's." John took his arm away, he turned to go.

Will stopped him. "What about Mary May?"

"You don't need to worry about her," John said. "You may well see her soon enough. She is with us now. She is with us just as she is with her brother. Both of them are now a part of us."

SHE LOOKED AT DREW AND WAITED ON HIM TO SAY SOMETHING to her, but he never did. He just kept driving. They were headed down the mountain. All she could see when she looked out at the blur of forest as they passed it by was her own reflection staring darkly back at her.

"Where have you been?" she said.

He turned for a moment to look at her. He was now more man than he was boy and she wondered briefly when and how that had come to be. "I've been here and there," he said. "Working, I guess is what you might call it."

She sat and stared at him, she was scared to ask. "Working?" she said.

"They've been good to me up here."

"That right?"

"That's right." He glanced her way again then put his eyes back on the road. "You don't trust them, do you?"

"We were raised not to. And some would say for good reason, too."

"You're talking about Daddy and Mamma, aren't you?"

"Who else," she said. "John and them have been scaring off our distributors. They've been trying to shut us down."

"You still selling alcohol?"

"Not much of a bar without it."

"There's reasons for what they do. There's good reasons."

She shook her head. "You sound just like them."

"There's good reasons for that, too," he said.

They had come down the mountain about five miles and he

turned the wheel. The truck tires came off the pavement and she could hear the gravel beneath the tires and small rocks hitting in the wheel wells.

"What's this?" she said. "You said you'd take us home."

He looked over at her but did not say anything. She leaned forward now and peered ahead, trying to decipher their route from the darkness.

"I said I'd take you home," he said. "I didn't mean your home, or Mamma's and Daddy's home."

Up ahead she could see cement blocks to either side of the road and the gate there. The gate now opening to take them in. Church members waited on either side and she could see the guns they carried and the eyes they laid upon her as they passed.

She sat there watching them as they went. And as Drew brought the truck forward, she turned and saw that same gate close behind her. "Drew?" she said.

"Don't you worry."

She reached behind her and brought up the .38, holding it at her side just out of sight.

She could see buildings now and lights and the spire of a church. Outside the night seemed to grow darker as they drove, the lake there only distinguished from the night by the reflection of their headlights. She could tell beyond the buildings and the church the land was a mix of trees and grass that came up from the lakeshore and rose toward the mountains.

Drew pulled the truck around and brought it to a stop. He leaned forward and brought the transmission into park, then he took the keys. The engine stopped working and for a moment she felt very alone there in the truck, as if her brother were not there, and she had been left now completely on her own.

"Is that Daddy's .38?" Drew asked. He turned now and looked to where she held the gun, then he looked to see what she would say.

"It's his."

"I wondered if he still had it."

"You wondered?"

"I just thought about it sometimes. I've thought about a lot of things while I've been up here."

"I wish Daddy would have found you," she said. "I wish he'd had a chance to talk to you."

"You think it would have changed some things?"

"I think it would have. I wish you two could have worked it out."

"He never really gave me much of any kind of chance," Drew said. "You know that just as well as me."

She studied his face in profile. "He was stubborn but it didn't mean he didn't care."

"I get it," Drew said. "Look, they put this place aside for you." He nodded toward the little house that sat before them. "You'll be able to shower. You'll be able to rest. I'm sure you're tired. I'm sure you could use a little time."

"Time for what? I never asked to come here. I don't want to be here. I want you to take me home. Not here but home. Our home."

"There's people who want to meet you, Mary May. You under-stand you are a guest. They only want to talk to you."

"They can come into the bar if that's what they want," she said. "We're open every day from noon to two."

"You know what I mean," he said. "I don't want you being rude."

She gave her brother a hard stare. "You know they shot at me? You know they shot at me just this afternoon?"

"I think that was just a misunderstanding," Drew said. "They're good folk up here. You'll see."

She didn't take her eyes off him.

"Look," he said. "Don't shoot no one. They want to talk to you. That's not going to hurt you none. And when it's all done you'll go back down to Fall's End and your bar."

"And you?"

"What about me?"

"You should come back to town with me, Drew. That's what Daddy and Mamma would have wanted."

"That's kind of you to say, but you and I both know there's not much truth in that."

WILL RODE IN THE BACK OF THE PICKUP WITH THE FOUR OTHER men. All of them were thirty to forty years younger than him and tattooed and pierced in ways that Will had never even thought of. None of them said anything to him, but he could see their eyes rest on him and on his rifle from time to time before they moved on again, back out to the forest beyond and the night that now came on toward them forty miles per hour at a time. No one talked. The wind was rushing with a fierceness as they came down the highway road then turned down the gravel lane and came to Eden's Gate.

John rode shotgun and Will watched him lean and talk with one of the guards. The guard bent down to talk with John and then pointed out ahead of him to where the buildings sat.

It had been three weeks since he'd been here and he could see the metal fence posts were beginning to go in at the perimeter of the property. A new house was going up as well. One of many smaller houses that made up this community, some still unpainted, half salvaged and half built of roughly sawn wood and plank that had been erected down the gravel drives that composed this place. There were fires burning in many places and he watched the people who stood around them, men and women, some he knew by name but many he didn't.

The driver took them down through the houses and small outbuildings and Will looked toward the pickup he thought he'd seen Drew driving. It sat in front of a small house with white clapboard siding and a single light on within. He could see nothing of the inside through the curtains save the light.

"Is she in there?" he asked, turning to the man who sat closest to him.

The man only nodded, the pickup coming to a stop now just before the church.

John was up out of the truck, and he came around thumping his hands along the top of the bed. He gave Will a pat on the back and told him to follow him.

They moved back through the compound until they found the square tractor barn that had sat there always. John led him inside the aluminum-sided barn that sat atop a wood frame and that served as the mess hall for all of the compound.

"You'll see some things have changed," John said.

It was dark in many places and their feet rang out in the emptiness of the place as they walked. Above, lights hung from the rafters, a chord suspending a single bulb within the green cone of a shade. All of it gave the place a washed-out tone. In one corner, leading down and then out of sight were the collected pipes and wirings that provided water and electricity to the houses and church.

Will kept walking. He followed John a little farther and he was led among a collection of long wooden picnic benches. John told Will to sit.

Like much of the place seen at night, this place was poorly lit and he sat and set his bag down then put his rifle atop the table.

John had disappeared through another door about three quarters of the way down one wall of the converted tractor barn and Will put his eyes upon it.

He did not wait long before the door opened and a woman came out carrying a tray of food and a glass of water. He knew her almost as soon as he saw her and he stood and watched her come toward him across the floor.

He took off his hat and she leaned in and looked at him then set the tray on the table right between them. "That's some of that buck you shot last week. Thought you might appreciate it."

He thanked her and waited for her to sit before taking his own seat across from her. "You eat already?"

"Yeah," she said. "They have it all set up like clockwork around here. That there in front of you is almost the last of it. It doesn't take long for us to get through just about anything these days. All these new faces around here and all of them young and hungry." She watched him dip his fork into the meat. It had been cooked slow and he could see they'd put some fat to it.

When he looked up at her she was watching him. "How are you doing, Holly?"

"Better than I was outside this place."

"Uh huh," he said. He ate some more of the meat. She'd put a slab of cornbread on the side and it dripped with butter. He picked that up and ate it too.

"I like to watch a man eat," she said.

"Well, I like to watch a woman from time to time too," he said.

She smiled at him. "You're still a charmer, Will. But old as you are I doubt you got much left in the tank for me."

He smiled back at her then picked up his glass and drank it halfway empty. She was nearly thirty years younger than him and for a time she'd been his closest neighbor. But her husband had beat on her and Will had gone over there almost weekly just to check on her and see that she was okay. After Will's wife and daughter died he had not seen much of Holly for four or five years, then one day she just showed up at the gates of the church saying her husband had disappeared, but Will had always thought Holly had been the one to make him disappear.

"John said maybe we'd be seeing more of you now that Lonny's gone," Holly said.

Will coughed and put a hand to his mouth, almost choking on the meat. "Word travels fast," Will said.

"John just told me. He said Lonny had himself an accident. I can't say I mind that he is gone. He was an asshole to begin with. Always trying to fuck every single one of us."

"That right?" Will asked.

"That's right," she said. "So you think you'll start to come around more often? I've got to tell you it's starting to get a little weird."

"Weird?"

"Yeah," she said, lowering her voice a little. She leaned in now and looked him in the eye. "I fuck John from time to time and he tells me shit. He tells me shit I shouldn't hear. I don't have a fucking clue about half of it, but the other half is fucking out there. The Father and his scripture and all this shit about the prophet and the coming fire of Hell. Sinners and saints. Salvation and damnation."

"That's nothing new," Will said. He finished off his plate of food then pushed the tray a little way across the table. "That's just what passes for conversation around these parts."

"You're a hardened old cowboy," Holly said. "I always liked that about you. But just be careful you don't become an old fool like so many other fool men I've known."

He looked at her and she didn't say a thing. After a while, he said, "Tell it to me then."

Holly looked behind at the door she had come out of. Then she turned and sat a bit straighter in her seat. "Where to start," she said. "Guns, weapons, most of these kids my age and even younger on this shit they're calling Bliss. They suck it up their noses. It helps them do the things they have to do I guess."

"What kinds of things?"

"Most of them would kill their mothers if it meant they could get another hit. But the shit they're pulling on these farmers out here, on people we used to know, it's shameful," she said. "It's not the kind of scripture either of us remember from back in town. They'll find your weakness and then they'll start to push. They push and push and they keep adding on the weight. Eventually one thing has got to give."

He looked at her and waited on her to tell him more. "You still a believer?" he asked.

She laughed. "You are asking me? You? The one who would rather spend three weeks out of every month alone in the woods trapping rabbits and hunting bucks than sit here and have a conversation with another human being."

"We all serve our purpose."

"Yes, we do," she said, smiling at him. "Yes, we do at that. I believe in The Father. I believe in what he sees. In his words and what is coming. But sometimes—" She stopped. Behind, heard through the kitchen door were footsteps. She stood and took the tray up and as she turned Will saw John step through, then pass her by.

"You want anything else, Will?"

Will raised up his hand. "I'm done," he said.

"Good," John said. "You're going to need your strength, The Father asked to see you alone in his church. He wants to put his hands upon you and thank you personally for all you've done."

• • •

MARY MAY SHOWERED. WHEN SHE WAS DONE SHE DRESSED herself in the clothes her brother had left for her and she came out into the small living room where Drew was waiting.

He stood when she came in.

"I'm glad you found me," she said.

"I'm glad I found you, too."

She looked around. It was a small place, the living room and kitchen all one room.

"You ready?" he asked.

"I don't want to," she said. "I think we should just get out of here. Go home."

"You're a guest here, Mary May. Our parents always taught us not to be rude." He looked her over like he was waiting for her to say more. Then he said, "Don't be rude."

"MERCY HAS BEEN GIVEN TO MANY ONLY AFTER THEY WERE MADE to suffer. It was their lot to suffer. It was a choice. A conscious decision. Into this chasm they walked and the darkness closed in about them and only through their faith did they find salvation, walking forth from that chasm unharmed."

Will opened his eyes as soon as he felt The Father's hands leave his shoulders. He had been led into the church by John and then told to kneel. Alone he had waited there, looking about the place. The symbol of the church seen in every window and a large American flag hanging down the front of the church with the cross and rays of Eden's Gate there at its center amid the stars.

The Father had come in shortly after, his steps sounding on the wooden floor before he came and stood in front of Will. He wore jeans and a shirt buttoned all the way to the collar. Like all the rest of his congregation he was bearded, and though he looked much like his brother, John, he was a little taller and a little wider through the chest and shoulders. His hair was pulled back behind his head and his eyes met Will's and held him while he talked.

"Life has tested you, Will. You must believe that now. You must believe that you're here for a reason. Chosen for the good of our kind. There are dark times ahead. Dark times to come and we shall be like a light in those dark times."

"Yes," Will said.

"When your wife and child were taken, you were tested. You were tested once more today." The Father dropped down in front of Will, elbows on knees and his face so close that Will could feel the spit on his skin and smell the man's breath when he spoke. "The time is coming—the end of days. The air itself will be afire. And I will call my people closer. I will call them all to me and I will ask them to make ready. For we, like the pioneers who came to this country before us, will have a journey. And now I ask you, will you be ready for this journey?"

"Yes," Will said.

He rose and looked down at Will. "You have helped us, but we will need you even more. We will need the eye that looks down upon the people through the scope. We will need the hand that holds and swings the knife. We will need the finger that pulls the trigger. Do you understand, Will? Do you understand all that I am asking you to do?"

Will hesitated. He looked up at The Father.

"Many times in humankind's long history have we not trusted in our faith. And many times that faith has been tested. And so it was for all who have made the choice to undertake this journey. A journey of salvation, but a journey also of necessity—for if you are unwilling to take this journey you will perish. And now, Will, that time has come and I am asking you again, as I asked you in that long-ago time when you first came to us, are you ready to do what it takes to find salvation?"

The Father stopped. He walked a few paces away from Will before turning back. He waited for some response. But Will would not look to The Father.

"After your wife and child left this earth we feared for your life," The Father said. "We feared that you had let the weakness overtake you. But you did not. You became the hunter not the hunted. You gave up sin. You gave up vice and all the evil that had overrun your life. We put our hands upon you and together we took away your sin. We cut it from your chest, just as every member here has also given up their sin."

Will nodded. He thought about it now. The tattoo. The razor. The giving of the sin. When he looked toward The Father again, he said, "I remember."

HE WAS RISING FROM HIS PLACE JUST BELOW THE ALTAR WHEN Mary May entered. She stood at the back of the empty pews. A feeling of doubt began to slowly work inside her like a sickness spreading through every vein. She watched him rise and she watched The Father gather him up like the man was part and parcel of his family.

She recognized him almost in the same instant. She knew him as the man who had stood upon the rise. The tracker. The man who had shot at her and nearly hit her. The feeling that had begun to spread its roots within her body now suddenly bloomed upward through her head. She had made a mistake in coming here. She had made a mistake in letting down her guard. And maybe she had even made a mistake in trusting her brother.

When the man turned and walked their way, Mary May was standing next to her brother, Drew, and she watched the tracker come toward her. He was bearded and his face was worn and weathered from years of sun. Crow's-feet like cracked clay sat to either side of his eyes and the hair atop his head was patchy and going gray. She stared at him as he moved and his eyes flashed on her and for a second he stopped and nodded to her and said, "I'm glad to see you, Mary May." He said the same thing to Drew, then he took his hat that he'd been holding in one hand and squared it atop his head.

He was gone, out through the front door a second later and she took a step to take him in again, but Drew stopped her, holding a hand to her elbow where she stood. "Will Boyd," Drew said, speaking to her in a whisper.

She remembered the man. She had gone with her own family to the funeral of his daughter and his wife. A car accident if she remembered right. Will standing there alone as people filed past. Her own father and mother leaning in, reaching to hold him, and Mary May thinking now about how even then he had smelled of booze and of something sweet like salt and sweat and the turning of a body into something other than what it once had been.

She'd thought him dead, but it was obvious to her now that he was not.

When she turned now to the front of the church, The Father was waiting on them. He raised his hands toward them, and he called to them, saying, "Come, my children. Come forward."

Drew moved and then waited for her in the aisle. She walked with hesitation as she came to the aisle, taking her time to turn and then go on toward The Father. She could remember him, too. He had changed little but to grow older, and she remembered how he'd come up from Georgia years before, attending church in town with them and speaking to the congregation as a friend. He had offered the word of God when asked to, and he had sat in silence and quiet study as the pastor had spoken and it was not until months later that there had been the split between them. The Father, or at that time Joseph, had gone his own way, telling all that wished to follow that he alone could be their savior.

Now he stepped forward to look upon her. "Come," he said again, his hands outstretched, his eyes unwavering as they, too, reached toward her.

She came forward and soon his hands held her by her shoulders. He brought her close and she could smell his sweat, feel the strength of his arms and the way he gripped and held her to him like they had both endured these past few days only to finally find salvation together.

"I welcome you," he said. "I welcome you here to us, even as I have only begun to understand what has happened to your father, and to your mother."

She nodded. Her eyes now on the floor.

"Drew has said much to me about them. He has spoken to me and to us all and in his stories, and in his remembrance of them they will live eternal."

She nodded again. She did not know what to think of this. The way he spoke now seeming so different than that of his younger brother, John.

"Kneel now," he said. "Kneel and I will give you the blessing of my hands and together we will prepare to wash the sin from inside you, scour it from every bone, from every piece of gristle. You will see that all will soon be right in this world. All shall be good, and your place here shall be in a place of wakefulness, and my eyes shall look after you as one of the blessed children of Eden's Gate." He released her and stepped back.

It felt to her as if he had been holding her for years. She looked now to her brother where he stood not far off. The Father beckoned Drew to come closer. Then he told them both to kneel. Drew knelt first, and though her nerves were jumping within her skin she knelt as well.

"Good shall be the salvation of your body. Good shall be the giving up of sin." The Father gave his attention to her once again, putting his hands on either side of her temple. The warmth of his skin pressed to hers. "You are a sinner," he said. "You are a sinner and in your eyes, I see wrath and envy, I see guilt and shame. I see every deadly sin there is and I offer you salvation. I offer to help you put the trouble of your soul to rest." He fell now to his knees and without releasing her from his grip, he put his forehead to her own. "I ask that you hear me now," he said. "Hear me. Hear the call of Eden's Gate. I call upon you to listen. You are not alone, Mary May. You have sinned, but you are not alone. You have not yet been forgotten."

He began to pray, his voice lower, a shift of octaves that seemed to resonate now from down below. His voice rising as he rose, bringing his hands up, bringing her up within his grip. He called for her forgiveness. He spoke of alcohol. He spoke of sin. He said that she did not know the things she did, and that she, like many in this county and in this world, only asked for pardon. But that it was their souls that cried up from the darkness, not their waking voices. He said that she was like many more, that she had come to him and come to this church as only the first sign of a greater need. "Thank you, Mary May," he said. "Thank you for coming forward. I thank you, and your brother thanks you, and in this we offer you salvation."

She looked up at him. He waited now, looking on her with the same eyes that never seemed to blink. Sweat stood out on his forehead. The feel of his hands still pressed on either side of her.

"Do you accept us, Mary May? Do you give up sin as your brother has before you? Do you recognize the weeping of your soul and the call of its release from the body that has thus far punished it?" He released her and pushed her backwards.

She almost tipped over, but he was faster and he held her again, righting her and asking, "Do you give up sin? Say it, Mary May. Say it and all will be forgiven. Do you ask for the washing of your body, for the purifying of your soul?" He pushed her away again and she faltered but did not fall.

Now he walked away from her. He turned his back to her and looked upon the flag that hung there. She had for some reason not fully taken it in until he brought her attention to it. It was an American flag, but altered now, amid the blue and amid the stars she could see the woven thread of the Eden's Gate symbol. Almost a star itself, a cross fitted with many rays.

He had begun to talk, but this time softer, his voice slower than it had been, more deliberate, as if maybe he were channeling some other person, someone long deceased who had come now to take possession of the living. "Fire will be the ending," The Father said. "Fire and the destruction of all who have not yet washed themselves of sin. Fire and the hand of wickedness." He turned and waited. He let the silence linger there between them, and then as if coming awake from out of some dream, he asked, "Do you give up sin? Do you ask salvation of the redeemer? Do you ask to be washed? To be purified? To be forgiven and reborn?"

Do you . . .

Do you . . .

Do you . . .

She watched him. She watched those unblinking eyes. And she understood there could only be one answer.

OF COURSE WILL HAD BEEN DRUNK WHEN IT HAPPENED TWELVE years before. He had been drunk most of his adult life and losing them had made it no better. He tried not to think about them anymore. He tried to think of them like they were ancestors from another time, family long forgotten, kin in some way that had given him influence in some unknowing but completely necessary way.

It was The Father's words that had released this from inside of him. And as he lay there in bed, he tried to summon the spirits of those long dead that he had loved, he knew that without a doubt they were the reason he was apart from church and town, alone still even after he had given up his sin.

He rose and put his feet to the floor and looked in the dark to the sliver of light beneath the door. They had given him a room in one of the houses with two single beds and he could smell the lake through the windows that were open. The night air at Eden's Gate always seeming to move and drift like ocean currents in the liquid depths.

By the time he had pulled up his pants and laced his boots, he had thought too much about his wife and daughter. He could feel the tears welling in the dark and how they brimmed and then fell across his cheeks and stung his skin.

He was the messenger of his own demise. Twelve years had passed since he'd lost his wife and daughter. And he'd never been more certain of the part he'd played and the pain he'd caused himself and the ones he loved. He had bought that drink. He had sent that bullet flying, just as deadly and accurate as any shot Will had ever taken. But he knew it now for what it was, and he recognized it as a self-inflicted wound.

He pushed out through the door and stood in the empty hallway beyond and looked one way then the other. He did not know what time it was and he did not care. He needed air. He needed to see the stars and moon and to stand in the grass and see the night as he had grown accustomed to it in all his time out there hunting for the church.

And though he always wished he could go back in time and do it better, he knew that change would never be. He had bought that drink for the man who killed his family. He had sent that man out into the world as accurate and straight as Will could have made it, at that time, on that road; on that exact night when his wife, Sarah, had finally said enough, not trusting Will to come home on his own, she had put their ten-year-old daughter, Cali, in the passenger seat and drove to get Will from the bar.

Will had tortured himself thinking about the part he'd played. Even now he could feel this emotion he had come to know as guilt as it welled within him and rose into his throat. He swallowed it down like he'd swallowed it down so many times before, then he stumbled down the hallway, like the old drunk he'd been, and now knew he might well be still. He stumbled on, trying to overcome his own guilt and sadness. He went out past a small living area and into the open night air, and he tried to somehow gather the pieces of his life together.

He walked away from the compound and passed several guards who looked his direction but gave no greeting but a nod. When he had seen the stars and looked across the lake toward where the hills began on the opposite shore and the mountains stood darkly sitting, he turned and came back again.

A small campfire had been made close by the lakeshore and he came to stand just beyond the light, looking at the woman who had no doubt lit it. When he stepped out of the darkness and into the pool of light created by the flame, Holly only glanced at him before looking back down within the fire.

"You have trouble sleeping, too?" Holly asked.

"Something like that."

"There is truth in what The Father says. Though it is easy in the dark waking hours of night to question." She nodded toward a section of log that sat a few feet off. "You should sit. I'll be the one to bring you back tomorrow, now that Lonny's gone."

He thanked her. He watched the flame dance, then he said to her, "How does The Father know the things he knows?"

Holly laughed. "You mean, is he clairvoyant? Psychic? God's own prophet?"

Will just stared at her. "I mean how does he know? How does he know beyond a doubt?"

"No one knows beyond a doubt," she said. "God gave Adam and Eve paradise and even God could not keep them from using their own free will."

"You sound like him," Will said.

"Like who?"

"The Father. John. Every one of us. Man or woman."

"Adam and Eve?"

"I guess so," he said. "Is this paradise?"

"It is whatever you make it to be," she said. She looked at him now and laughed. He was starting to get the feeling she was in on some joke that he had no idea about. "Be careful, Will. They might not see what's going on with you, but I do."

"Is that what's keeping you up?" Will asked, offering her a weak smile, trying to defuse anything he had set in motion inside her head.

"I'm waiting up for John."

"How serious is this thing you have with him?"

"Serious enough to have me out here waiting," she said.

He looked at her. He looked out into the night. He wondered about the woman he saw before him, and he wondered about the woman he'd known before. He thought that they had been the same, but he did not know now if they were. "You get lonely up here sometimes?"

"It helps to have someone," she said. "It helps to keep the mind from wandering too far afield."

He looked at her. Holly pushed at a log with a stick and they both watched as sparks kicked up in a flurry then rose in the thermals. He wondered who she had been talking about, her or him.

MARY MAY WOKE IN THE DARK. HER BROTHER HAD NOT TAKEN her back down to Fall's End like he'd said. She had been given the little room in the little house and she had stood there and watched him, this man that was her brother but now somehow was not. She did not know him. She had thought she did. But she knew she did not know him anymore.

"You'll drive me back to town, won't you?"

"Yes," he'd said.

"You'll come with me."

"Yes."

"Don't leave me," she said. "Stay here. Stay right here in this house till morning. You can stay on the couch and you can drive us into town in the morning."

"Yes," he'd said.

She stood looking at him. In that moment, he reminded her of the little brother she had once had. She thought of their mother nagging on him. She thought of the answers he would give. Yes. Yes. It was always yes.

When she woke in the dark she knew she was not alone.

"Drew?"

Across the room she heard a rustling. A shift of fabric then the creak of a wooden chair beneath human weight.

"Drew?" she called again.

"Yes," he said. "Yes. I'm here."

She put an elbow down then turned and tried to see him in the darkness. He was a shape only, a shadow among the darker shadows of the room. "Is something wrong?"

"No," he said.

She could hear him shift. She heard him stand from the little wooden chair she remembered had sat beside the door. "Is something wrong?" she asked again, listening still and watching the dark shadow where he stood.

"You need to wash," he said.

"Wash?"

"Yes. You need to wash yourself in the water. You need to cleanse yourself. You said you would."

"Drew," she said. "You're scaring me."

"There's no reason to be scared," he said. He took a step now, and he came toward the bed then moved up and along the side of it.

Out of instinct she pulled back. She sat up and put her hands out in front of her like she might fend off whatever this might be.

"Don't be scared," he said again. "You need to wash. You need to cleanse and prepare to face your sin."

He had come closer now and she looked wildly around. She looked for anything she might use to stop him but there was nothing there and before she could move another inch, or throw up a hand, he had grabbed one of her ankles and turned sharply, pulling her from the bed with a savage tug.

She came off the bed with her arms flailing, reaching for anything that might stop her fall. Nothing could be found except for the bare sheets, and she fell two feet from the bed and landed on one elbow then hit her head.

The pain was instant and reverberated down through her skin all the way through her body. She had hit hard and fast, and she could barely think except to know she was being dragged across the carpet. She turned and bent away from him, reaching out with her hands. Her fingernails dug for purchase but came away with only dirt and sand and lint and whatever other thing that could be taken underneath her nails.

He swung open the door and the light flooded inward. She could see that he would drag her past the frame and out the door. She called his name, but he did not stop and she reached and grabbed the leg of the chair then the doorjamb as she went. For a second she held on, but he kicked her then brought her up again, lifting her by the ankle so that she spun and twisted with her head dragged backwards across the floor and out of the little room.

"Drew!" she said. "Drew!"

But it was as if he didn't hear her. He kept moving and soon they had crossed the living room. The door came open in his hand and she was yanked out after him and then let go.

She laid in the dirt and gravel of the drive. Small bits of sand against her face and in her hair. She coughed. The taste of blood from some cut she must have had inside her mouth and she coughed again then tried to look around.

John sat there waiting for her. He was sitting on the tailgate of a pickup truck and as she looked around, she could see the faces of many more. Men and women she had seen that day, church members.

"Hello," John said.

She turned and got a hand behind her and tried to sit. "What is this?"

"This is the end," John said. "This is what I've always wanted for you. You have been alone. You have lived without the word of The Father and now you will be alone no more."

She tried to push herself up. She tried to fight them when they came for her. She tried to rip her arms away from their grip. But there were too many to defend from. Soon she was in the air, carried up out of the dirt and thrown down across the truck bed.

She called her brother's name. She repeated it again and again, but she never heard any response.

Every one of us should be reminded how very alone we are when we indulge in sin and live without the faith that keeps the devil from our door.

—THE FATHER, EDEN'S GATE
Hope County, Montana

When Will woke Holly was sitting there on the single bed opposite his own. "You ready?" Holly asked.

"Yeah," he said. "What time is it?"

"Morning time." She had no watch to check and no phone, for there was no service even if she had one.

He pushed back the blankets then brought his feet over the edge and placed them bare upon the floor.

"Jesus, Will. You make your own underwear or something?"

He looked down to the briefs he wore. They were old and had once been black but years of washing them in the river then hanging them in the sun had turned them a sun-bleached brown. He looked up at her and smiled. "They're just a reflection of my life."

"Underwear are the windows to the soul." She sat up and told him to shower and then meet her in the barn cafeteria.

He showered then dressed in his old clothes. They still smelled of the mountains, of pine and dirt and cracked rock, and of his own sweat and salt. He carried with him his rifle and backpack as he came into the cafeteria and found her waiting for him.

She gathered up a basket and put it out on the table before him and told him to go through the clothes within. "I tried to find things that I thought would fit."

He looked in the basket and removed the first layer of clothes and set it to the side. "Where did this stuff come from?"

"Donations," she said. "You know how it works, Will. You come to us and you donate what you have and we give to you as well. We are a communion, though I never would have called it by some hippy shit name like that."

He picked through the clothes and found the ones he thought would work, and then he rolled them and put them down within his bag. "There's more of this?"

"Sure," she said.

She brought him into the long room that took up half of one of the houses and flipped on the lights. He saw the piles of clothes that stretched from one end of the room all the way to the other. There were piles of shoes as high as he was. There were gloves and hats in another pile. There were coats, pants, shirts, underwear. He walked along down the middle of them all. There was little order to it other than by article—children's clothes thrown in among the adults. He stopped and picked up a children's size eight set of shoes by the shoelaces that connected them. The laces white and stained with dirt, while the shoes were pink and purple.

He looked back at Holly where she stood. "The Kershaws? Lonny said they had brought them somewhere. They had a daughter and a son. But I've seen no children. In fact, I haven't seen the Kershaws, either." He stood with the shoes dangling in his hand and he ran his eyes out across the piles of clothes then back again. He was beginning to see items he recognized. Shirts that advertised the local little league team, or one that showed the emblem of the lumberyard. "What is happening here? Where is everyone?"

"I see where your mind is going, Will. But you don't need to worry. They are with us. But they are not with us here."

He held the shoes still. They were like something he'd once had in his own long forgotten life. "I don't understand," he said.

"There are other places being set up," Holly said. "There's a woman out east who runs our farms. She grows our food, she gives us the produce we need. The eggs. The meat from different live-stock. Surely you didn't think it was just you. The church is every-where and there are many to feed," she said.

"And that is where the children are?"

"Yes," Holly said. "Everyone is safe. Everyone has their purpose. You'll see one day."

He dropped the shoes now and he looked around at the piles once again. "There's so much," he said.

"Jacob, their oldest brother, has also begun to train women and men in the mountains."

"The mountains to the north?"

"Yes," Holly said. "Not far off. There's much that has changed. And I can see now that Lonny did not keep you up to speed as he should have. We are growing, Will. You and I are some of the first. But many have started to come and ask for our protection."

"Protection?"

"Yes," Holly said. "From their own lives, just like you. Just like when you came to Eden's Gate and gave up the bottle and gave up sin. Others come because they need financial help. Others come because they have lost the faith. But, regardless of how they come to us, they all need our help. Souls do not save themselves," Holly said.

Will watched her. He looked once more across the piles of clothes, then he turned to her again. "I think I'm ready," he said. But he could see in her face that she had unsettled something within him, and that she knew it.

"We're building toward something here," Holly said.

"I know. I get it. I can see that now." He grabbed his bag then took the rifle and put the strap over his shoulder.

She led him out of the room and they came out of the small, wooden clapboard house into the morning light. "Throw your bag back there," she said as they came to the pickup she must have pulled around earlier.

He put the bag into the bed then walked to the door and pulled it open. No one was about and only far down the drive, past the small wooden houses and outbuildings, did he see another soul. Two guards stood at the gate and he watched them for a time and watched the weapons on their shoulders.

When he opened the truck door and climbed inside, she was waiting for him and she turned and cranked the engine. "It's been good to see you, Will."

He looked over at her. He still held the rifle and he settled it now between his legs. "It's been good to see you, too, Holly."

She pushed down on the pedal and they went on down the gravel road. "You really shouldn't be a stranger anymore, Will. Even when you're here once a month you are a stranger. I can see that now. I'm going to make sure I come and see you. John asked me to. He asked me to be the one to keep track of you now that Lonny's gone. I'll be coming by."

"I'd like that," Will said. He wasn't looking at her anymore. He was looking at the houses. Many were painted crudely white, like the church behind them. Others were simply rough wood, stained to keep the weather out. They kept driving and his eyes landed on one and he could not take his eyes away. In big painted letters that had run and dripped down the white siding was the single word, SINNER, written across the front, just beside the door.

His head moved to take the house in even as they passed and he turned in the seat and watched as the house receded behind them. He could not remember the same word being there the day before. He turned back now and looked out the front windshield, but in the side mirror he could still see the house and he watched it and then when he turned to say something to Holly, she instead began to speak.

"It's been weeks since you've been here last," Holly said. "You should come once a week at least. If you're with us you should come to the Sunday services, Will. You should hear The Father's sermons. The way he speaks. The power of his thoughts and the message he gives to us from deep within his soul."

"I will," he said. "I have missed too many."

HOLLY LET HIM OUT IN FRONT OF THE GENERAL STORE IN TOWN and he thanked her and climbed from inside the cab and grabbed his bag. When he came back down along the truck she called out to him through the open window of the cab. "You sure you don't want me to bring you all the way up to your place?"

"No," he said. "I need new snares and new traps and I need some more cartridges for the rifle. Most of my snares are probably gone by now, torn up or dragged clear across the fields."

"Okay," she said. "And you'll get a ride with someone going up that way?"

He nodded. "It's no trouble. Thank you, Holly."

She looked at him for a time and then leaned to the open window. "I'm trying to help you out here," she said.

"I get it. I'll be okay on my own."

"That's what I'm getting at," Holly said. "I've been trying to tell you how things are changing. Eden's Gate, The Father, John, all of it. I see you and I worry about you, Will. You're going to get left behind or pushed aside if you don't start making the effort."

Her talk had riled him up a bit. He didn't like being told what to do, or to have his actions questioned. "Like you?" Will said.

"Yes, like me, Will. I might not like everything that's going on up there but I know who butters my bread. I can see you still making your mind up about that."

Will cracked a smile. "Well I'm not going to start sleeping with John if that's what you're asking."

"Fuck you," Holly said. She wasn't smiling about it and she put her hands up on the wheel for a second and looked on down the road. When she turned and met his eyes again, she said, "I might not agree with everything they do but I owe them my life. And you owe them yours. You understand? I might criticize them but I'm on their side always. It's your choice, Will. I already made mine."

She opened her mouth to say something more, but instead she simply turned the key and started the engine again.

He stood there for a while, feeling a little dumbfounded, as he watched her pull around in the street then head back the way she'd come. He felt bad about what he'd said to Holly, but there was nothing he could do for it now.

He went inside the general store and bought his cartridges and a couple hundred feet of twenty-four-gauge snare wire. He bought needle-nose pliers and wire cutters because his had started to rust from the use he gave them, working in the open with the rain and snow that saturated the fields every spring and winter. He put everything on the tab that Lonny had set up for him a while back, and he thought now whether Holly would know to pay it for him. He was standing at the counter when he thought about the bear cub and asked the clerk about the beaver traps and the small floats that went along with them. He bought five and he came out of the store with most of it stuffed down inside his bag, and the traps that he could not fit strapped along the side.

He walked to the end of the block then stopped and stared into an empty window. He placed his hands to the glass and peered inside: dust and empty booths and barren tables. There had been a café here only a year before and he wondered now when it had closed and where the people who had owned it had gone. He walked a little more, then crossed the street. The bar sat there in front of him, just the same as it had always looked.

He walked up and saw the beer lights were off, a "Closed" sign sitting in the window. He set his bag down to the side of the door then walked along the outside. He could see only shadow and outlines of things through the dark windows. He stood there and thought it through. He was no fool and he'd never been one.

Holly had told him that Mary May and her brother had come down that very morning and he had sat and thought about that and he had thought about the fresh paint he'd seen there on the side of the small house. Wondering the whole while if it was the same house he had asked about the day before—the house in which Mary May had been.

Will also thought about how the bullshit alone could only be piled so high before one thing or another broke beneath its weight. He turned and looked back across the town. He saw that many of the buildings were boarded up now and he remembered a time when every one of them had been open and behind every door and every window was a business or a neighbor. He did not know when that had changed, and he did not know when he had stopped noticing, though he certainly noticed it now.

He put his hands to the window again and tried to see inside. There was nothing to see except his own mirrored face looking back at him. He moved back to where his bag sat. He put a hand out and tried the door. It was locked. He stepped back a little, turned again and walked the length of the bar and then, at the corner, he went down the side of the bar and came around the back.

There were trashcans there and a storage shed and halfway

down he saw the wooden service door. He walked past the trash-cans and tried the door. He was surprised at first when he found it was unlocked. He still carried his rifle with him and he took it off his shoulder now and held it in his hand. In no way did he think that he would use it, but he also was aware that he was going into someone else's bar, that there might be some consequences for his actions.

He cracked the door and looked in on the kitchen that sat just behind the bar. Close by, just at the point where the white linoleum ended, he could see the wooden barroom floor. He could see chairs atop tables and the shadowed light that was let in through the dark-ened windows.

He could hear voices now and he stopped with his hand still on the doorknob. Inside and very close there was a man's voice and then, softer now, a woman's voice responding. Will leaned and pushed the door open then went inside.

Sitting at a stainless-steel prep table was a man, stocky, wearing a white chef's coat, stained in many places. Just beside him, around the adjoining corner of the table was a young girl, who Will guessed could be no more than twenty-one. Both turned and stared at him, their conversation cut short.

The chef stood and Will shifted and moved the rifle, but then thought better of it, knowing now who stood before him, "Hello, Casey," Will said. "You cook here now?"

The cook, who had been a few years behind Will at high school, took a step then stopped just at the head of the table. It was obvious he was still trying to determine what this was. A half second passed while the girl looked to Will then back at Casey. Finally, Casey said, "Will?"

•   •   •

THE ARTICLE WAS ON THE FRONT PAGE OF THE LOCAL NEWS-
paper. A paper that held little content usually, and that most in town
stockpiled and simply used as fuel for their wood-burning stoves.
The back section of *The Chronicle* was for selling tractors or fly-
casting lessons, and the front section was mostly just pieces regard-
ing the local weather, or the annual log jamboree, or what was going
on that week at the VFW. Casey handed him the paper. He stood
behind the bar and Janet, the waitress, sat a couple stools down and
looked Will's way.

"Saloon owner found dead," Will said, reading the headline of
the article aloud. He looked up at Casey. "Gary died?"

"Irene died two weeks before him."

Will's mind raced. He was thinking about them both. Gary and
Irene. They were parents to Mary May and Drew. They were the
owners of this bar. They were friends, or they had been until Will
had gone and disappeared twelve years before.

"Last week we had the funeral for Gary," Casey said. "A week
before we had one for Irene. They're out there in the cemetery, side
by side. The grass hasn't even had a chance to root."

Will read the article. He looked back up at Casey then looked
down the bar to Janet. "Where's Mary May?" he asked. "Or Drew?"

"Drew?" Casey said. "We haven't seen Drew in months, maybe
even longer."

"And Mary May?"

Janet spoke up, she was watching Casey as if maybe she should
get permission, but then she ran her eyes to Will and said, "We
haven't seen her in a couple days. She closed the bar. She said for
us to come back in and see her today and that's what we were doing
when you came in. We were waiting. We thought maybe it was time
to get back to work."

Will looked from Janet to Casey, then he turned and looked

around the bar. He hadn't been in here in twelve years, but nothing that he could see had changed. The same dark paint, wood paneling, and beer signs, the same dust in the corners of the room.

He brought his eyes back around on Casey. "Gary and Irene are buried over at the cemetery? The one here in town?"

WILL LOOKED DOWN AT THE GRAVESTONES. HE HELD HIS HAT IN one hand and his rifle in the other. The earth had barely even sunk in, mounded and fresh there atop the graves. He scanned his eyes out across the rest. Names he'd known. Names he recognized. He stared off toward the two he knew, his wife and daughter. It seemed to him that this place was dying. It seemed to him that every soul he'd known was here.

"They asked for help but no one listened."

Will turned now and saw the pastor standing there. He was dressed the same as Will had always remembered him, in his black suit and white collar. And though there was white in the black curl of his hair, he was younger than Will by at least twenty years. And, as far as Will remembered, he'd been a gunnery sergeant in the first Gulf War before he'd found God and then brought his faith here.

"*I* did not listen," the pastor said, as if he wanted to offer clarification for his sin.

Will ran his eyes across the man. The cemetery sat before the church and behind, seen across the graves, a single door was open and Will could faintly see the pews and window glass beyond.

"I thought maybe you had come to burn me down, to harass me, and to hurt the church. But I think now that you are here to see for yourself what your church has done. And I wonder now, seeing you here again, whether the things you see before you have left the same mark on you that they have left on me."

"Jerome," Will said. "How are you?"

"Tired. Mostly tired all the time now. Mostly sick and tired of the shit that goes on."

Will had taken his backpack up as he'd come out of the saloon and he'd walked the length of the town with the rifle held in his hands. He held it still and he looked Jerome over and said, "I didn't come to shoot you, or harass you, or to burn you down. I came for answers."

Jerome laughed. He was not prone to it and he looked at Will and said, "Eden's Gate has many answers. The Father has many answers for those who seek his shelter. But I do not have the answers. I am not the prophet The Father wants us to believe he is. I am a follower of God. I am a reader of the Bible. I do not change the words to suit my own delusion."

"Christ," Will said. "Can you cut the shit, Jerome. Cry havoc and let slip the dogs of war on someone else."

"People love to quote Shakespeare right before they go to war," Jerome said. "It probably makes them feel pretty smart just before they get their ass blown off and start to feel real stupid. What the fuck can I do for you, Will? You want to confess a sin?"

"Maybe several," Will said. "For now, I just want you to tell me what happened here."

"Irene died a few weeks back. It's going to sound sappy as hell, but I truly think she died of a broken heart."

"How's that?"

"About a year ago your buddies started to come down pretty hard on Irene and Gary. They made it clear they didn't want them selling alcohol. They even stopped a few trucks that had come out this way on delivery. No booze meant no money. And no money meant they had to make a choice between giving up their house or giving up the bar."

"They chose to keep the bar?"

"You know it," Jerome said. "But guess who swoops in and buys the house for pennies?"

"Eden's Gate."

"You're quick," Jerome said. "It was like there was no one else who was even willing to buy the place. They could offer whatever they wanted for it and they knew Gary and Irene would have to take it."

"And Irene?"

"She's dead a month later. It was an aneurysm or something. A pressure in her head."

"And Gary?"

"We tried a few times to get the word to Drew, but you know how Eden's Gate can be. You know they don't listen to a thing we say. Gary just decides he's going to go up there. He's going to get Drew and bring him down here so we can do the funeral for Irene."

"That's not how it worked out though, is it?"

Jerome stared back at him. He looked down at the two graves then back up at Will. "What are you playing at here, Will? You still with them? You said you came here looking for answers but it seems like maybe you already know each and every one. Let's cut the shit. One vet to another, you want to tell me what the fuck is going on?"

"I'm starting to realize I had half the story," Will said. "It seems like you had the other side."

"You and I both know that's how it's always been with war."

Will looked at him. "Irene and Gary used to mean something to me," Will said. "Their family meant something to me. I was a mess but I knew that."

"Things change, Will," Jerome said. He raised a hand and gestured to the graves that sat everywhere about them. "This place is testament to that."

"Yes, but they had family—all of them. You forget that sometimes in war. You forget about home. You forget about the people there. You and I both know what that's like," Will said. "You're out there. You're so far away from all you know that it starts feeling like your life out there is your real life, and the life you knew back home, the normal one, the place you were born, the place you grew up, that's the fake life, the false life, and mostly all you want is to be back at war."

"Is that what you want?" Jerome asked. "Because I'm older now. I'm smarter. I can tell the difference. I'm not blind the way I used to be. I'm not fool enough to think it's one reality or the other. They are the same. This life and that life, they're all just one big fucking mess. Most everyone here knew that in the end." He stepped past Will now and looked out on the cemetery.

Will thought about what to say. He thought about Mary May and he thought about how she'd gone up there and found her brother. "You're a man of God," Will said. "You ever seen the word 'sinner' painted on a house?"

Jerome's eyes came around fast. "Where did you see that?" he asked.

"It was painted on a house up at Eden's Gate. I'm trying to remember if it was painted there the day before."

"I've seen it," Jerome said. "I've seen it written on a couple houses close by Eden's Gate. The owners came to church right here in town and they both were trying to sell their houses, but they could never get anyone to buy. No one wants to live next to a place like Eden's Gate. No one wants to be neighbor to a cult. Both families just went and left one day. They just left and they never said a thing. They didn't even sell their places. I guess they figured they were worthless. I heard later that Eden's Gate bought them from the bank."

"And you went there?"

"I went there after they didn't show up to church a couple Sundays in a row. The places were empty, not a piece of furniture, or a strip of clothing. Just empty. Someone had tagged up the houses and written 'sinner' on the side for anyone to see."

Will turned and looked upward on the sun. He wondered when it was that he'd last seen Mary May. He wondered how much time had passed and he hoped he was not too late. When he looked back over at Jerome, he asked, "You got a car or something I can use? I need to get back up to Eden's Gate."

"Then you are still with them?" Jerome asked.

"Never farther from them, actually. You can call me stupid for saying this but it's probably time we cued the Shakespeare."

MARY MAY CAME AWAKE GASPING, AS IF SHE HAD GONE TO BED beneath the waves. They had done something to her. They had given her some drug.

She was in a dark room and though she was awake, her vision swam and then refocused, colors seen at the periphery of her vision like that of some negative universe. Black was white and red was green. They had left her in a corner and from where she sat with her back to one wall and her head leaning against the other, she could see the sliver of light that came in from under the door and reached across the floor toward her. She tried to move, but her hands had been bound behind her and as she tried to wriggle free, she realized her fingers had gone numb.

They had bound her legs at her ankles and as soon as she tried to stand she fell and hit her forehead against the floor. She could smell dust, and something metallic, something that seemed now to remind her of the metallic taste of blood.

With her feet she pushed away at the wall then inched across the floor, her eyes moving out ahead of her, searching out the light. Her hands and fingers had started to come to life again and there was the prick of needles across her skin and the warm fuzz of blood now coursing in the veins. She pushed again, inching closer.

They had taken her in the truck and left the compound. All the while sitting around her where she lay. She had tried to get up many times and been knocked down over and over again. The feel of the road beneath the tires, the bounce of springs, and the smell always of the pine that had surrounded them and moved above, branches blotting out the stars and moon. When they stopped she knew they had come to a river rolling down out of the mountains. The air had changed and had become cooler. The smell was of water and silt and rock. And farther out the sound of the rapids running and the water flowing, ever faster.

She did not know yet why they'd come for her. She did not know yet where her brother was. She had looked around as they brought her up and dragged her by an arm from the truck. They threw her down in the sand right there at the edge of the water.

"Do you confess?"

She tried to find the voice that now addressed her. John stood knee deep in the water, and he walked forward now and held a hand out and cupped her chin within his palm.

"Do you confess?" he asked again.

"Confess what?"

"Do you confess your sin?"

She looked up at him in wonder. There was a sense, though fleeting, that none of this could be possible. There was a feeling inside of her that this could not be real.

"Confess and all will be forgiven," he said.

She looked wildly around her for her brother but she could not see him and she felt John's hand tighten against her chin. He held her there like that, his hand to her face and his fingers gripped upward across her cheek. "Where's Drew?" she managed now to ask.

"Drew?" John said, as if he had never heard the name. "Drew is all of us and all of us are Drew. You know little of your brother. And you always have, but you will see now what he is and what we are and in this you will find your own salvation."

He released her. He stepped back and raised his arms, as if he might be raising them to some rain now falling from above. "Those who walk in heaven are those who have unburdened their heart of sin," he said, his arms still upraised and his voice now thrown forth among them all, Mary May and everyone who had taken her and held her down in the truck bed. "Those who are unburdened may walk and hold the hand of the prophet. Those that have been unburdened can enter into heaven. But those who choose to go against his mercy, those who do not reveal to us their sin, those that would turn their back on Eden's Gate and all its providence, those few who have not the foresight to understand, they will be cast into the hell of their own making. The fire that will come and scour the world to ash and flame."

Slowly, he brought his arms down then moved his eyes again to where she knelt. "Now, brothers and sisters we must help her—help her to find the way."

She could feel around her the movements of the people. She

could feel them tightening around her. She was having a hard time breathing, as if in their movements they had also sucked up the air. She started now to hyperventilate and to fight with every breath for oxygen. They closed in on her and two lifted her beneath the arms and carried her toward the water. She was fighting now, moving arms and legs and she could feel her toes dragging in the sand, cold and wet and heavy.

They went into the water with her and to her side she saw a man begin to pour some dark liquid in among the current. The liquid riding on the surface like an oil and the smell of flowers coming to her but no flowers seen anywhere in the dark flow of the river.

"Now, brothers and sisters, you all know the process and the reasons why. We come here to complete this process and I hold you all responsible to witness and to support the wishes of salvation given to us here tonight. Mary May is a sinner and we will be the hand that cleans her of her sin."

She felt John's grip wrap around her neck and she was pushed forward and her head went down within the oily water and then was left there. She struggled, fighting in the inky black. She kicked and fought, but they held her on both sides and she could feel John's nails digging and holding to her skin.

She came up sputtering. She spit away the water, and she had almost no time to scream. She felt his hands still there behind her and then his voice again. "This one fights against salvation. This one fights to keep her sin. And you see, brothers and sisters, that there is a demon in her. An evil that tries now to evade the good will we give to her, bestowed upon us by The Father. Well, she will learn there is no fighting. She will learn to accept her sin and then in that way lose it. She will learn that my hand and your hands are the tools of the prophet and the prophet's own extended power."

He dunked her again, and then held her. She could feel the liquid drift beneath her, she could feel the cold. She did not fight this time, fearing he would not let her back up again. But now, as the seconds ticked by, her body began to convulse and she could not control her own urge to breathe and to free her mouth and nostrils from beneath the liquid. She fought and he held her down below.

She woke in a dark room, gasping for air as if they had drowned her. Which she knew now they had almost done. Her clothes were still damp and she inched forward now, moving across the floor with hands and feet bound, inching toward the light.

JEROME TURNED HIS ANCIENT OLDSMOBILE OFF THE COUNTY road and down the double track that ran atop the bluff. Will had told the pastor all he could think to say, but he knew there were details and minutiae that he simply did not know, and he was realizing even after he'd told his story to Jerome that he had let both Eden's Gate and The Father blind him. And as they came out along the bluff and saw the lake and the buildings of Eden's Gate below across scattered stands of forest, Will knew that though he'd found the light to see Eden's Gate for who they truly were, he was still blind to so much more.

"You tell me where," Jerome said. "I still think this is craziness and I still think you might be crazy."

Through the trees, with the Oldsmobile moving, Will saw fleeting glimpses of the buildings. He scanned ahead to plan some course for himself that would bring him down off the bluff and hide him as he went on foot to find Mary May and bring her back. "Go up here a ways and when you find cover stop the car."

Jerome turned and raised himself up to better see the land below. "That's a lot of ground to cover."

"I have the rifle," Will said. "I'll be fine. I'll keep them at a distance."

Jerome pulled over then brought the car around. There was a grouping of short pine that sprouted from atop a nurse log. Jerome sat there for a little bit, then he cut the engine and looked across at Will. Jerome's face was completely serious. "You know they have guns, too?"

Will just looked at him and smiled. "Yeah," he said. "I heard it's kind of their thing."

"That worry you at all?"

"It only worries me if they start using them."

"I can go with you," Jerome said. "I certainly could help."

"You are helping," Will said. "If she's down there, if they have her, if we can make it back here, we're both going to need you ready to get us out of here."

"Okay," Jerome said. "Try not to get shot at."

Will cracked the door then moved to get up and out of the seat. "It's not like I haven't been shot at before," Will said.

"Getting shot at is fine and dandy," Jerome said. "Getting shot is not. You remember that one and try to make it back here."

Will closed the door. He carried his rifle and settled his hat down across his head. He had taken his hunting knife from within his bag, and he had loaded up his pockets with the .308 cartridges he'd purchased that same morning. He went down through the trees now and when he came to an opening that looked out toward the lake and Eden's Gate beyond, he settled in and put the lens on them and watched to see who might be watching back.

•   •   •

SHE THOUGHT THE LIGHT AHEAD WAS DAYLIGHT, BUT THE CLOSER
Mary May came to the sliver beneath the door the more she started
to doubt that. She lay on the floor and with her hands behind her
and her ankles bound she could only see the slightest movement of
air there before the door. Bits of dust floated like protozoa in some
languid current within the sea.

There was the sound now of echoed footsteps. They kept coming closer as if they were moving down a long and very empty hall.
The steps came closer and her eyes bore down on the splinter of
light that sat before her and soon she saw the shadow move across
the opening then come to a stop in front of her door.

When the door came open the light was blinding and she
clenched her eyelids together and tried to turn away. There was
little escape to find and she rolled as far as her hands would let her
and she lay there and watched the room come into focus. It was a
room of standard size and on every wall she saw the writing of the
sins. The seven of them repeated hundreds of times, each on a different set of faded, almost wax-looking paper pieces that had been
pinned to the wall somehow.

Gluttony.

Lust.

Greed.

Pride.

Envy.

Wrath.

Sloth.

Mary May rolled and stared at them from where she lay, looking
every scrawled word over. The papers jagged and misshapen where
they were not pinned. She kept looking at them and then, startled
and in a rush, she realized what the smell of this room had been.
The metallic, almost vinegary tang of skins stretched one end to the

other and pinned by the hundreds across the wall. Dark to light like every color of the human body.

"You shouldn't worry," Drew said. He stood at the door looking in. He waited as her eyes adjusted and her vision cleared.

She rolled now and looked to where he stood and she saw his eyes running over the walls then dropping to where she lay.

"In the wilderness after you fled into the forest John had wanted to kill you. He had wanted you to go away, to disappear. I asked him not to kill you. I asked him to spare you as we have been taught to spare all that see the truth." Drew came forward into the room. He studied one of the skins a little way down the wall, then he turned to her. "This one," he said, gesturing to the skin. "This one is my own."

She looked to the wall and read the sin written there, Envy.

"The Father and John helped me to see that I was envious. That I had always been envious and that it would continue unless I accepted myself for who I was. They helped to strengthen me, and in the process they showed me how lost I had truly been."

"That's yours?" she asked. She did not understand. She looked at him and then around the room. "What is this?" she asked. "What are those?"

He bent and knelt in front of her. He reached a hand out and touched her neck then ran his fingers down across the sternum of her chest. "They tattoo you right here," he said. "They look into your soul and they see the sin that you are carrying and they bring it to the surface when they tattoo it across your chest." He stood again, taking his hand from where it had pressed down on her. "Once you accept your sin, you can then release it." He hooked a finger up and pulled down the collar of his shirt.

She could see the scar tissue there. Almost as if it were a burn, but she knew it was more than that—that the skin itself had been removed. She looked to the wall again. She looked to the sin that had sat atop her brother's chest. When she looked back at him, she said, "What have they done to you, Drew? What have you let them do to you? You're not this man. You're not the man they think you are."

"No," he said. "I'm not that man anymore. You're right about that." He took the .38 from behind now and he brought it up and stared down at it like the gun itself were some treasure rescued from the bottom of the sea. "They never treated me like an equal. They never thought I could ever be anything like you, or like him. They always thought I was lesser. They never wanted me. I know that now. I know it was their sin that gave me life and I accepted that. I accepted them for that and for what they did when they gave this life to me. But they, in turn, never accepted me."

"What are you talking about?" she asked. "Mamma and Daddy loved you. He came up here to get you. He came to get you and bring you back, just as I did. You have to see that there is love there. You have to understand that."

"No," Drew said. He brought the gun around. He held it out toward her now, and he reached and pulled her to her knees. "You are the one that doesn't understand. You are the one who has been marked with sin. Who needed to be cleansed. I am the one who has saved you. I am the one who saves you still."

She listened to him, but what she heard most distinctly, and what terrified her all the more, was the sound of another set of footsteps now approaching down the long hallway.

WILL HAD COME DOWN THE BLUFF, WORKING ALONG THE SLOPE at an angle. By the time he reached the flatlands near the lake he could see the buildings through the trees and he pictured himself there among them. The trees were patchy in many places and his view looked toward the lake and among the trunks of the trees and though Will was one of them he knew he must be cautious in his approach. He threw himself down among a growth of thick underbrush and glassed the compound.

He had a straight shot to the house where the word SINNER had been written, but in its place now was white paint. He ran his eye across it several times before he was even sure of what he saw. The word was gone. Erased as if it had never been there to see at all.

Using the scope, he viewed the gravel drive then moved the scope along each building. He had little idea where to start or even to guess where he might find Mary May or in what state.

When Will had come to the church twelve years ago, he had come to confess his sins. He had come to speak to The Father and to ask him for his forgiveness. And while Will had always been a believer in the church in town, he had prayed to them and his prayers for peace and for acceptance of the things he'd done, had, in his mind, gone unanswered.

The Father had told him to have faith. He had laid his hands upon Will in a way so different than Will had seen, or felt in town. The Father hugged him and brought him toward him like a brother. Gesturing in that moment to his own brother John, and the eldest among them, Jacob, he had said to Will, "You will be to us a brother, and that bond you share with us will be even stronger than the one we three share even in our blood. You will be family to us and we will care for you as family and you will care for us as family and in this we will take comfort and provide for one another for the rest of time."

Will had been released and he had stood there with The Father, and with the ten or so followers that soon would grow to become many hundreds. And Will had looked back at him and The Father had said for him to bathe in the water of the river and to immerse himself and wash his sin.

John, himself, had been the one to baptize Will. And afterwards he had said to Will, "Now you must confess. You must confess your sin."

"But I do not know it," Will had said.

"You know it. You know it just as you know your own reflection seen—but then forgotten—in the passing of a mirror."

"I cannot see it," Will said. "I am lost. I am lost without them, without my wife and without my daughter."

John had pulled him close just as The Father had, and he had led him to the edge of the river, bringing him to a tranquil eddy where the water sat calm and still. "Now you see the sin inside you," John had said. "You are a hunter. You are a killer. You are a man of Wrath and not of good. You are here for this very reason. You are here to appease your sin and erase the Wrath that lives within you."

Will dropped the scope from his eyes. He knew now where they had taken her. He knew now what had been done to her and he feared now he might be too late.

JOHN CRADLED MARY MAY BY THE BACK OF THE HEAD. HE BLEW the powder upon her, and then he knelt and looked inward on her. It seemed to her that he was looking through her, in through the eyes then out the back. The powder roiled within her like a smoke, pouring past her eyelids and down her throat.

"You only had a taste of the true power of the Bliss in which we bathe the sinners," John said. "You did not have the chance to see the world in its truest form, stripped naked, and revealed." He stepped back now and watched her. She was having trouble keeping focus. A cloud was moving across her vision and all she saw had morphed and begun to pull. Still, she was aware that Drew was standing with her, their father's .38 still held in his hands, the gun barrel pressed upon her skull.

"There's no need for that anymore," John said. He told Drew to lower the weapon. He told Drew to cut the rope that bound her hands and feet then to step back and stand behind him.

She tried to move her arms and to get her feet beneath her, but she felt weighted in place as if she were made of stone. Her arms dangled now like the air itself had become a gel and she had dove headfirst into a world composed not of any solid conglomeration of atom or particle, but instead into a world made loose by the breaking of many different bonds.

She moved but also did not move, and afterwards, when her mind had time to catch up to the instinctual manifestations of her body, she wondered even if she had ever moved, or if, as she felt now, with John looking down upon her, whether she were even still within her body.

"I'm sure Drew told you what I'd wanted to do to you," John said. "I'm sure he told you that I thought you might be better dead. But I think it's better this way. I think it's better that you know that he still loves you, even if you do not give to him the very same. That is why we marked you. That is why we brought you to be washed. And now we ask you to confess so that we can send you back as one who is marked with sin but not forgiven."

Her head swam, and she tried to still it on her shoulders. Everything was out of focus and even as she looked up to John and Drew, she could see they had begun to almost melt from off their bones.

She turned her gaze upon the wall. The skin hung all around her. Stretched and pinned with staples like long dead butterflies beneath their case. With the drug now streaming full through her she thought there was a kind of beauty to it. A kind of beauty to the sin and the skin that hung there, that had been taken from off the sinner's chest.

John turned and spoke to Drew. He said the next part would not be easy for a loved one. He told Drew to go back to the house, to wait. He said this all would be over as soon as he could get her to confess.

There was hesitation seen, but then acceptance, and soon Mary May was aware she was alone with John and that as the door closed behind Drew and John stepped forward into the overhead light, he became a figure of some form that was only shadow. In her eyes it was the figure of her own father she saw looking down on her.

It was her father. She was sure of it now. And when he pulled back into the light she was certain of it. His face. His eyes. The touch of his hand across her cheek. Mary May could not understand it. She watched him move away from her and walk the full length of the room, and for a long time he didn't look away from her. It is him, she thought. It is him. Her mind was trying to make sense of it. She now felt the drug in every vein.

Her father rounded back to her. He took her hands into his, and he leaned and turned each palm upward. His eyes searching out the whorls across her skin like he meant to create a map of the maze that was her fingerprint. Now he began, his voice stopping and starting. And the voice she heard was not John's but that of her dead father, addressing her as if to give her comfort from the afterlife. His words carefully chosen, as he spoke and paused, drawing some words long while cutting others short.

"Your hands," her father said. "Look what you have done to them—look what you have done to them just to be here. They are bruised and cut. They have been wounded, misspent, and misused. You came to us and though you might not see it now, you came to us in order to receive your purpose. And that purpose starts with these hands. The things they might build. The creation they might make. There is so much potential in just one of these fingers. In ten there is an infinity."

There was a showmanship to this. A resonance that was somewhere between tent revival and southern Baptist snake handling, and Mary May was trying to understand it all. She was trying to make sense of this being she saw before her, John or her father, and she could not distinguish between the two. She listened to the rise and fall of his voice, and she wondered about a thing like the afterlife and whether a soul could cross back in time of need, and what that soul in all its infinite knowledge of life after death would see in her— whether she would be declared saint or demon, burned or saved.

He looked her over. He looked up and away from her to where the skins hung pinned against the wall. And in her mind the skins were moving and there was the sound of them rustling on the wall like snakeskin, spent already from the body, artifacts that showed the secession from one state of being to the next.

She didn't believe it. She didn't believe it was her father. There was no coming back from death. He was gone. He was gone from here and this could not be him.

John brought his eyes back to her. The gaze he cast upon her was almost predatory, like a cougar looking out of the darkness at its prey. The realization of where she was and who she was with and the danger she was in suddenly came rushing back to her. She tried to pull away, but his hand held hers firm in his. And when she looked down it was not John's hands she saw but her father's once again. Aged and callused. Loved. Hands she could not hate. Hands she wanted to hold to, as if holding to them would prevent him from ever leaving her again.

And when she looked again he was caressing that hand of hers like a father might the broken hand of one of his children. "Together," he said, his voice now tender. "Your hands in mine, in the greater fold of this family there is only warmth, only understanding, only the true gift of potential we see for you. But without that gift you are alone."

He held her fingers for only a beat longer before he dropped them. What he said to her was true, she felt the cold of the room. She felt the decay in the air, not just skin, but dust, and loss, and solitude.

"Do you understand?" he asked. "Do you understand your sin, and the way it stands before you, blocking you from the gates of heaven?" He stood now in the light, his skin illuminated from above, her father. His hair seemed almost gossamer. She looked around now, as if coming out of some dream into the waking world, knowing the feel of danger, but not seeing it. She could see only her father and she wanted very much to go to him and to hold him and to never let him go, but she felt weighted to the floor, as if she were in the water still and he was looking down on her from the breathing world above.

He began to speak again. "This sin will govern you from waking moment to your final half-remembered dreams. But I can stop it for you. I can bring it toward the surface and then someday cut it from your skin. Will you do this willingly?" he asked, waiting now on her reply.

She looked around the room. She looked from skin to skin then back again to him. Her father had faded away but no one had taken his place, not John or Drew, or anyone. What she saw there was no longer human. He was a voice above her like that of some god speaking from atop the mountaintops many thousands of feet above. "Yes," she said.

He seemed to reset and his voice began to roam about the room, and she was having trouble tracking it as he went. "What beautiful things are the gifts of hands. They are gifts given to all of us. They are like the tongue, or the mind, or the muscle beneath your skin. They are a tool and they have been misused. Chipped and bent, marred, even broken a time or two, but they can heal. They have this power and it is a power not to be forgotten. For all the bad those hands have done, for all the paths those hands have wrongly led you down, for all the days those hands spent in toil only to find you were building an effigy to a false prophet—those hands can still be healed. They can be tools again in the way they were first intended."

He came back to her now, the drug fading a bit and she saw it was John there before her and not her father. He held her hands again. She was scared not because of where she was or who she was with. She was scared of the words he used and the way they had begun to seep inside her and bend and harden like scaffolding meant to support and soon overtake her very being.

"I am glad," John said. "I am glad Bliss has released in you this path to a truer understanding." He guided her hands now to where her collar was and he began to pull with her hands in his, ripping the material of the collar until she felt the bare skin of her flesh come exposed in the dead air. "Your sin will go here above your breasts, and it will be a mark for you to remember us by. You will have many days and nights to think on it, and in the end you will find there is only one conclusion, and that conclusion will be that you will join us here, giving up your sin, and your life beyond. But first we must prepare you. We must wash you clean, for your sin is envy, and it will be placed upon you for all to see."

•   •   •

WILL LET HIMSELF IN THROUGH THE FAR DOOR THEN STOOD looking down the long hallway with the overhead lights in cages every ten feet or so, six of them in total and the doors of the rooms beneath each. He had not been here in years, but he had not forgotten this place. He knew where the room was, and where his own tattoo had long ago been stapled to the wall. He knew this was where they would take Mary May. He knew it because he had once been taken there himself.

He had gone only a couple of steps down the hall when he heard the opening of a door. He came to a dead stop and then, thinking fast, he ducked into the nearest room. With the blackness of the room behind he stood there with the door just cracked and a slivered view of the hallway before him. He wondered what would happen if he was caught here, whether they would be able to see he had lost the faith. He wondered whether it was that obvious, and whether they would have come to his own house to write the word SINNER upon his walls.

In what little light there was Will slid the rifle bolt down and checked the chamber, then carefully pushed it back into place. He listened to the soles of heavy booted feet pass by then fade again.

Will cracked the door a little then eased out. Going down the hall was Drew. Will watched him walk, his movements almost robotic. Each step labored and deliberate, one in front of the other all the way to the end, where he let himself back out into the light of day.

When Will heard the door close, he went again into the hallway. Will had not liked what he had seen and he wondered now why Drew was not with Mary May. Will started to doubt himself, but he also feared for Mary May all the more.

He held the rifle out before him and began to walk in the direction Drew had come from, heel then toe, the rubber beneath his boots softly echoing. If she was here she was down this hallway. He looked ahead and continued, his eyes fixed now on where he thought she'd be.

There was a creak of door hinges then the sound of footsteps up ahead. A voice was heard suddenly. A voice Will knew was John's.

Will moved fast. He took three steps, trying to keep the sound of his own boot soles hidden. The inlaid shadow of a door sat before him, and he ducked in just as he saw John come into sight fifty feet ahead. He was talking to someone, but Will's own pulse had begun to beat so fast and loud in the channels of his head that he could hear nothing. He had felt this way before. With the big boar grizzly, with his own wife and child, and before all that he had felt this in the war. Now he tried to push this feeling down away from him and loosen its grip from around his skin.

When he bent and looked again around the inlay of the door, John had turned and moved away in the opposite direction. Will saw him open a new door and then disappear within. Will was out and moving down the hallway. His heart still beat inside of him with a thump that shook the skin, but he kept going. He moved because he had to, because he thought there might not be another time. If he was going to save Mary May this was the only time. He only hoped now that he would find her and that whatever had happened to her, wherever she was in the process, was not now at its end.

He came down the hallway with the same fast and silent steps. He reached the door that held the sins within, and he turned the knob now and pulled it open. Mary May was there before him, kneeling on the floor five feet in. Her eyes were glassy and almost nonresponsive as he moved to her and tried to bring her to her feet. The collar of her shirt had been ripped and pulled aside and he could see the beginning of her bra and the naked upper skin of her breastbone. He tried now to gather the material up, to somehow help her.

"Mary May," he said, whispering to her then turning to look behind him. He had left the door open and he felt the cool air of the hall flowing in like a ghost unseen. He turned back to her, he tried to bring her up and to get her on her feet but she was unmoving. He snapped his fingers in front of her. "Mary May, you need to help me. We need to go. We need to get you out of here. We need to get away from here. You don't know the things they do."

She turned her head slightly, and then she met his eyes. "Are you up there?" she asked.

He was watching her. Mary May's eyes swam beneath her lids like something come loose from all that anchored them, but her voice had stunned him for a moment with how clear and deliberate she had made it sound. He turned again and looked behind him and when he came back to her, he said, "I can lift you. I can lift you out of here and carry you over my shoulder. But if you can walk and help me it would be better. We may need to fight to get out of here. We may need to run and I don't know if we will get away if it comes down to that."

Her eyes washed past him now. He tried to meet them as they went. He watched her head roll to the side then turn upward on the wall. "Are you up there, Will? Are you there on that wall with all the rest?"

"Jesus," Will said. "What did they give you?"

"Are you up there?" she asked again.

"Yes," he said. He looked around wildly, desperate to escape and knowing if he was found here that it could get no worse. "Can you help me? Can you help me get you out of here?" He did not wait for a response, he bent and lifted, getting her over his shoulder like some backwoods kill. He turned around and began to move for the door but she stopped him.

"Don't," she said. "Don't take me."

"What?"

"Don't take me. Put me down."

He paused at the doorway, cautious, not wanting to be seen. "What are you talking about?" he asked.

"John is only going to tattoo me," she said. "I came to get my brother. I came for Drew."

He didn't want to listen. He didn't want to hear what she had to say, but he knew even with whatever drug they'd given her, he knew what she was asking him to do.

"Put me back," she said again. "Put me back exactly as you found me." Her voice was so deliberate. Each syllable defined and clear. "If my family ever meant anything to you, put me down."

He turned and set her down.

She looked up at him. She watched his face as he stood watching hers. "Drew is at the house where they put me last night. He is waiting there. Do you know it?"

She was drugged and he could see it in every movement she made. But there was clarity there, too, like someone surfacing from a coma for a single moment before they were lost again. "Yes," Will said. "I can find it."

"I think they killed my father," she said. She said it almost as if it was an afterthought, but he knew it was not. He knew she had been thinking about it all along. "You need to be careful," she said. "I came to get my brother and I came to get him out of here. It's what my daddy wanted. Can you do that for me, Will? You were always one of Daddy's favorites. You were always missed even though we knew you were not gone. Not really."

Will turned and looked to the open door. He was losing time.

He might lose his life if he stayed here. He knew now what the members of Eden's Gate were capable of. He knew it was not Lonny alone who had wanted Mary May to die out there. "What about you?"

"John wants to tattoo me. He wants me to be marked so that he can in some way feel he controls me."

Her words were clear, but he could still see the drug working away at her. She had felt lifeless as a sack of grain when he had lifted her. Will turned again. He had to go. He kept his eyes on the doorway a half second longer, and then he brought the hunting knife up from where he'd put it on his belt. He turned back and lowered the knife down and hid it between the floor and her calf.

"You can't trust John," Will said. "You can't trust anything he says. You might need to get out of here on your own. You might need to use the knife. I'll get your brother, and then I'll figure something out. I'll try and come back for you if I can. The pastor from town, Jerome, is waiting with his car on a road to the northwest, up above the Eden's Gate property. I'm telling this to you because you might need to get out of here on your own. You understand me?"

She nodded.

He gave her one last look, then he turned and ran. Halfway down the hallway he heard the doorway behind open, and he dashed forward and hid again in the place he had before. When he peered back out, down the hallway, John was moving upward with his eyes on the doorway and the room within where Mary May waited. He held in one hand a medical kit and in the other he carried the metal surgical tray Will knew held the tattoo gun and ink.

•   •   •

She had moved not a muscle from the time that Will left to the time John came through the door. The only thing, she realized now, was that when John had left he had closed the door, and now as he came back in, it stood open.

She watched him move into the room then set his medical bag on the floor and put the tray down next to it. On the tray, she saw the tattoo gun and needle. Not far off, rolling slightly back and forth on the metal tray was the bottle of black ink. John turned now and looked toward the open door. He seemed to consider it for a time. And then he looked back at her. "You wouldn't move, would you? You'd stay still? It will make it easier if you just accept it. If you just accept the sin and let it happen."

"I accept it," she said. She had not moved at all and he looked her over then looked back at the open door.

"That's good," John said. "I don't want to ask anyone to hold you down, or to tie you up. It always goes easier if the sinner is willing. It helps me. It helps the ink and the writing of the sin."

He walked now to the door and stood there with his back to her. When he turned again and looked to where she knelt, he said, "Still. I don't trust you." He walked out through the door and returned in a few seconds. He held in his hand a metal stool with a swivel at its base that raised or lowered the stool up and down. He brought this toward her and set it on the floor.

Next, he brought the tray over and began to bring up swabs and alcohol from within the medical kit. When he had laid it all out he simply sat there on the stool. "I know you said you wouldn't move, but the needle always makes them move. It makes them move and I wouldn't want you to ruin the work I do." He stood and took from his pocket a vial of the same powder he had blown across her face. He uncorked it and blew it over her again.

The feeling washed over her as a wave might break upon an ocean shore. She was immersed in this feeling once again, dragged outward and away as the wave receded.

WILL WENT THROUGH THE DOOR AND INTO THE BRIGHT SUNLIT afternoon. He could not shake the feeling he should have stayed. He should not have listened to Mary May. They should be out here in the daylight, moving toward the bluff where Jerome waited for them both.

There was a real dread that Mary May would never leave this place. There was fear that John might be killing her even now, suffocating her, or otherwise hurting her in some way and Will almost turned and went back inside, hoping again that he was not too late. But he did not do it. She had been drugged, but she had seemed in control. She had seemed certain that what she was doing—getting a tattoo—was only a small sacrifice to make in order to free her brother from this place.

Will knew the tattoo was only the first thing though. He had looked at her and looked up at the wall on which all the skins had been placed and he, for a moment, had been terrified of just how many he had seen there. Hundreds more than he had thought existed. Hundreds more Eden's Gate members than he had previously known about. And though this meant he did not know them, it also meant they did not know him, and if anyone suspected anything of him, it would be his end.

He set off along the passageways that moved in and out of the buildings that made up Eden's Gate. He came down then circled out and around the backs of the houses that lined the gravel drive.

He kept low, one hand on his hat as he moved and the other hand carrying the rifle right there beside him.

He moved house to house, hiding at the back of each before sprinting across the open space that divided one from the next to come. When Will found the house he thought Drew was within he still could not be sure. Many of the houses were much the same and he walked cautiously along the side and came to the front. Down the gravel drive he could see the guards and up by the church he saw more men and women of Eden's Gate. On the road were several more and he stood with his back flattened to the siding then reached a hand out and felt the paint. It was drying in the place that SINNER had once been written, and his fingers came back white at each tip. The whorls of his fingerprints now cloudy with the paint.

He moved back along the siding of the house and as he went he wiped his hand down along his clothes. The paint was almost dry, but it came away in places and marked his clothes where he had put each finger.

When he got to the rear of the house again, he moved toward the back door. He stood in front of it for a time, and then he reached a hand and turned the knob. The door opened and fell inward with his hand still on the knob. He was careful now not to let it fall against the wall. He took a step inside and saw that the door led into a hallway. The bathroom sat on one side and a bedroom sat on the other. Out ahead of him he could see the kitchen and a part of the living room, and he was cautious as he went, for the light of day went before him into the darkness of the place and as he went himself, he cast his own shadow out before him and he could see there was nothing he could do for it but to continue.

Drew was standing with his back to Will, looking out through the blinds toward the larger building in which the tattooed skins were collected, and where he'd left his sister.

"Hello, Drew," Will said. He stood at the end of the hallway where it came into the living room.

Drew turned and his face was startled but not overly suspicious that Will was there.

"When you first joined Eden's Gate I should have talked to you. I should have tried to be around a bit more," Will said to him. "Even though I left town your parents always meant something to me, and so did you and Mary May." He walked a little farther into the room. He still held the rifle, but Will was no different than any other member of Eden's Gate who carried a rifle one place or another on this land. "I'm learning I should have been around. I might have been able to stop what happened to your father. I guess a lot has changed."

Drew's eyes darted to the small coffee table in the corner of the room and Will saw there a chrome-plated .38. When Will brought his eyes back he could see Drew was watching him again. "You come to kill me, Will?"

"No," Will said. "What would make you even say that?"

"For what I've done."

"You haven't done anything yet," Will said. "I can help you."

"You were friends with Mamma and with Daddy."

"I know that," Will said. "But that makes me only want to help you all the more. I loved them, you know. Your daddy and mamma were like family to me. I wouldn't want to hurt you or Mary May." He took a few more steps, and he watched Drew's eyes move again toward the .38.

"You don't know what I've done," Drew said. He moved now, going for the weapon there on the table in between them.

Will met him with a crash, lowering his shoulder and using the whole weight of his body to throw Drew against the wall. And though Drew was a half foot shorter than Will and probably fifty pounds lighter, the shock of hitting the younger man was felt all through Will's shoulder and down along his side. He watched Drew hit the wall then slide almost to the floor, but Drew was up again in the same instant and he dove and fell into Will, driving both to the floor.

They rolled and knocked into the table. Will heard the gun go over and the heavy thud of it as it hit the floor. Will's own rifle had been lost when Drew had hit him and Will now turned and tried to locate it and to find the .38, but he saw neither as he called out suddenly in pain.

Drew had struck him hard in the ribs with the knuckles of his fist. He hit him twice more in quick succession as Will rolled and tried to get away. Drew moved after him, both men scrambling and trying to get the better of the other. Will put a hand out on the couch and tried to lift himself, but Drew lunged and belted him across the back again and Will fell away, losing his grip on the couch and any chance he'd had for standing.

The effort had brought Drew to the floor again and while Will rolled and tried to keep outside Drew's reach, Drew came up onto his knees. As he was getting one foot under to stand again, Will got hold of the coffee table and flipped it over his body to where Drew knelt. The table hit Drew just as he raised an arm to fend it off and though Will knew it had not hurt Drew much, Will saw in the same moment that Drew had been thrown off balance.

Will got to his feet and charged. He came down on Drew with the same force he'd leveled on him the first time, throwing all his weight toward the man. They went to the floor in a thrash of fists and legs, rolling and hitting out at each other. But it was Drew again who managed to land a sudden hit to Will's head.

Will lay stunned, flat on his back. Drew got up and went for the gun. Will sent a foot up and across Drew's shin, tripping him and bringing him back to the floor. Now Will came to his hands and knees and grabbed out after Drew and gripped a piece of his clothing then tugged back.

The .38 lay just ahead of Drew and he reached for it with his hand. His fingers gripping into the carpet as Will grabbed and pulled again. Drew kicked back but Will managed to avoid the brunt, and now he got his forearm beneath Drew's chin. Will pulled up hard, bending Drew's spine upwards and cutting off his air supply. Drew's hands and fingers remained outstretched, searching for the gun while Will kept pulling back ever harder.

Drew, most likely seeing he was trapped, began to aim elbows backwards into Will's sides and lower chest, the majority landed poorly. Now, as Drew fought and Will maintained his hold, the smaller man started to dig and rip at Will with his fingers, scraping the flesh of Will's forearm and raking his fingers across Will's face.

Will just kept holding him and after a minute he could feel Drew begin to slacken. He held Drew for ten seconds more before he let him drop to the floor again. Will stepped over him then reached and pulled up the .38. He stepped back over Drew and stuck the gun down the front of his pants. Next Will dropped down on all fours and lowered his head to look beneath the couch, and then he put a hand out. His hand came back from underneath the couch gripping the rifle.

For ten seconds he stood there with the rifle strap over his shoulder trying to get his breath. Drew hadn't been able to hurt Will in the stomach, but the movements had brought the sourness of bile to his lips and when Will ran his tongue out he could taste the tang of blood. Something was coming apart inside him that he did not have the time for, and he looked around the room and knew this was not the time to dwell on it.

When he felt his nerves begin to still and his breath to even, he went to the window Drew had been standing at. He looked in the same direction he had seen Drew look. There were still a few church members up toward the church, but no one seemed to have noticed the sound of the struggle there inside the house.

Will crossed the room again and looked down on Drew. The man's chest was moving almost imperceptibly beneath his shirt, and his head lay to the side. Will bent now and lifted his hat from where it had fallen on the floor and squared it atop his head. He wished there had been time to reason with the man. He wished there had been more to say. He watched the movements of the chest. Drew had given him no other option and though Will had hoped they might just walk out of here, Will knew now that the only way he was going to get Drew up the hill and off the Eden's Gate property was to carry the smaller man across his shoulder.

Taking a knife from the kitchen, Will went from room to room cutting the cords from any electrical appliance or lamp he could find. He came back into the living room and trussed Drew's ankles together then his wrists behind his back. When he was done he rolled Drew on his side and, using the same kitchen knife, cut material from the couch then folded it and stuffed it down into the man's mouth.

Drew was beginning to come awake so he brought up the last bit of electrical cord and wrapped it tight around the back of Drew's head and mouth, and then tied the gag in place. When he stood again, he could see Drew's eyes had begun to flutter and as Will watched, he came awake and tried to free himself from the wrappings of the cords.

Will stepped away again. He could hear the man fighting it and he could hear his voice as he tried to speak and the muted call of his scream as he tried to free himself. Will didn't pay him any mind. Will could feel the fresh marks Drew had left on him, the nails that had gouged his skin, both across his forearm and across his face. Will also knew that one side of his face had begun to swell, most likely beginning to discolor from the punches that had landed on his cheek and neck.

When he looked out the window he saw the same things he'd seen before, but this time he looked toward the building in which Mary May was being kept. He watched the far trees and he thought about the mile or so between Eden's Gate and where Jerome was waiting. Will wondered now about Mary May and if he had done the right thing listening to her.

He came away from the window and without even pausing to speak to Drew, Will bent and lifted the man up and over his shoulder. Will guessed he weighed around a hundred and forty pounds and the weight of that first step nearly stopped Will in his tracks, but the next step felt a little better, and the step after was a little easier. He had carried full-grown bucks that weighed the same as Drew, but they had not been alive and they had not been fighting and Will now purposefully knocked Drew's head twice against the jam of the back door as they both went through.

"Don't fuck around," Will said, keeping his voice low. "I told Mary May I was getting you out of here and I'm going to do it. But we're going to get your sister first because you're heavy as fuck and I could use a hand."

He hadn't gone more than fifty feet when he turned and looked out between the houses to the road. Holly was standing there and it was as if her feet had been nailed right there in place. Her mouth was open like she was about to scream and her eyes were on him where he stood, Drew up over his shoulder, the rifle over the other, the .38 down the front of Will's pants, and the blood and bruises showing on his face and arms.

For a second he thought to tell her it wasn't what it looked like. But he knew it was exactly what it looked like. And just as she was about to take a step toward him, or to run screaming up the road to the church or to the guards with their automatic rifles, Will turned and ran, still carrying Drew atop his shoulder.

MARY MAY WAS COMING BACK INTO HERSELF. SHE HAD BEEN washed far out to sea and her head swam, then dived, and for a very long time it was like she was not within herself at all but floating somewhere in the deep below.

Now she began to feel the pressure on her chest. She smelled the alcohol John had used to wash her. The sting, almost like an electric current vibrating across her breastplate. John took the needle back, and now he leaned and wiped a rag across her chest then stood looking down upon her.

He sat again on the stool. She blinked then blinked again and tried to wash the haze from the surface of her eyeballs but whatever it was it seemed not to wash at all and she saw him lean again and place the needle to her skin. When she looked down she could see the tattoo was halfway done, the black ink showing on her skin and the raised lettering swollen and red around the edges.

"I'm glad we have this time alone together," John said. "I like to have time alone with all I mark."

She watched him shift atop the stool then run the rag across her chest again. There was blood seen there amid the ink and her head swooned a moment then recovered.

He began to work again, and she felt him move the needle down then bring it up again as he formed the letter V.

"Sometimes Bliss works to hold you inside your head," he said. "I've seen it do strange things to people. I've seen them hallucinate, and to disappear within the high. There is a common experience that they all tell me about afterwards, and that is of them looking up from down below. They are looking down a long path, or they are looking up as if from out of a well and if they can make it to the top they can make it back. But many have said to me they feared they might never make it." He ran the needle down the V again then brought it back up again. "You will make it, Mary May. I can see that in you. I can see you will be fine. And once you realize your sin. Once you see how it has been brought forth onto your skin, you will understand it better and you will come and ask for it to be severed from the body."

He bent and pressed the needle into her once again. He had started on the Y. The pain she felt was more acute and she looked around the room now and began to remember the reason she was even kneeling here. Her brother Drew had set this up. She thought of him now. She thought of Will. She wondered where they were. She wondered whether Will was coming for her.

There was pain now like she had not felt before. A dull, almost everlasting pain that seemed to hover across the top of her breast and to slip down and wrap itself around her bones. She turned and looked down on the needle, and she saw the word had taken shape. ENVY. Red and swollen was the word and her own blood rose red from among the black.

"Almost done," John said. He moved back again and wiped the cloth across her chest. He leaned outward and whistled in self-congratulation at his work. She looked again. The letters were two inches high and they spanned the center of her upper chest.

He wiped her again. Then, after appraising her a moment, he bent and pushed the needle once more across the wording, tracing each letter as he went. Tears were forming in her eyes and now she began to think of her hands and of her feet and there was a desire in her to get away, far, far away from here. Will had told her not to trust John. He had told her she might need to run and to get away. But he had also said he would come for her and she looked now to the door behind which John had placed his stool. The door was open and though she wanted Will and her brother to appear there they did not. She was still watching the hallway beyond when she began to hear the siren. Now, pausing in his work, John's head turned to better hear the siren, too. He stood and looked about, running his eyes out on the hallway and the place where the siren seemed to grow only louder.

He took a step out, and he was standing there in the hallway now. Mary May looked down at her chest. The letters were bleeding and as she tried to stand she faltered and had to reach a hand out and support herself with the stool. She remembered now about the knife tucked away beneath her calf and she bent and put a hand to the floor and, almost in disbelief, pulled up the knife and held it in her hand.

She could barely get her feet beneath her, but she knew she had to. She had to run. She had to find her brother and she knew now almost without a doubt that whatever Will had tried to do, escape or find her brother, he had failed at one or maybe even both. She put a hand out, tried for balance. John had disappeared, and she looked now to the open door. She tried to get one foot in front of the other, but both her feet seemed to be made of gelatin and her legs felt as wobbly as rubber bands.

It was as she tried to get her feet together that she kicked the vial of powder and saw it roll and then come to a stop at the edge of the room where the wall came down and met the floor. She stumbled toward it. Each movement pulling at her freshly tattooed skin. Her chest from her breasts to her neck felt like it was afire but she kept moving, keeping her eye ahead and on the little vial that now might offer her the only chance she had.

She came to the wall as if she had not expected to come to it so soon. She hit hard and slid, her one open hand bracing for the floor. In her other hand, she held the knife and now as she came to a rest, she moved her fingers outward and found the vial and brought it to her teeth. It was stoppered with a rubber cork and she bit at it then spit the cork away.

The siren was still blaring overhead, but she could hear between its howling roll that there were footsteps coming closer. She pushed herself up, and using the wall to steady herself she came to the door just as John returned.

"Where are you going?" he said. He was smiling, as if this were all some game she'd made for them, the siren blaring and the grin across his face.

The smile ended as soon as he saw the knife she was holding in her hand and, caught off guard, he took a step away. She jumped and landed on him, bringing him to the floor. She held the knife in one unsteady hand. For a moment only she thought to use it. But that moment passed almost as fast as it had come. Instead she bent and with her other hand she dumped the powder out, shaking it over him and across his mouth and nostrils. She watched the capillaries in his eyes bloom and expand, as if a star had burst suddenly into stardust and thrown itself across the sky.

She pushed away and rose now, running on legs that felt like rubber for the doorway far ahead.

•   •   •

WILL HAD TIME ONLY TO REACH THE HOUSE THEN THROW DREW
inside before he heard the siren. The whoop of it like some air raid
signal Will had only heard long ago as a kid.

He left Drew to sit there with his bound legs across the back
hallway floor, his spine against the wall. The house was the same as
he had left it, and he crossed now and went again to the window and
parted the shades. Out on the road he could see church members
moving but they had, at least not yet, figured out which way the
threat was coming from. Will turned and looked toward the guards
far down at the gate. He saw that two remained and the other two
were advancing up the road now, moving toward him.

When Will turned back again, he could see Holly there in the
middle of the road. She had likely been the one to sound the alarm
and he had to give it to her in some way, she had seen what was
going on with him, maybe before Will had seen it himself. Now,
as he watched her, he saw her point back to the place she had seen
him and Drew last, then she pointed roughly in his direction, sig-
naling which way he'd gone.

"Fuck," Will said. He let the shades fall and went back through
the house and stared down at Drew, and it seemed like Drew was
laughing at him. "I'm not dead yet," Will said.

He took the .38 from his waist, then spun the cylinder and
looked in on the bullets. Then he put the gun back in his pants and
crossed back through the house. He had seen propane tanks in one
place or another on the property. He went to the stove and turned
the dial on the range then watched the flame bloom red before
turning blue.

He looked around with a wildness and he had to tell himself to
calm his nerves and rein himself in a bit. He had to tell himself he
was going to get out of here, that it wasn't over yet. He left the flame
going on the range, and he turned and started to go through the

cupboards and all the drawers. He knew these people, and he knew their minds, their basic values.

When he came to the emergency candles he brought one up and looked it over, then he bent again and looked some more. When he found the cans of Sterno he set them on the counter. He took one from inside the packaging and pried off the top and looked at the flammable pink gelatin within. Not pausing any more he took a candle and dipped the wick through the flame then brought it to the open sterno. The flame bloomed almost purple. He looked around then brought the Sterno to the bathroom and closed the door.

He came back out of the bathroom and glancing down now he could see Drew's mood had changed. He was watching Will now with caution. Will took the .38 out again. He flipped the safety off, and he looked from Drew to where the flame still danced atop the range. He was adding time and distance up in his head wondering how they might even make it out of the house, or even up the hill without being shot somewhere along the way.

Will went back toward the front windows then parted the shades again. He saw the guards talking to Holly. He saw her point again in the same direction. The guards stalked off, their weapons raised as they went out of sight between the houses. Will looked down at the knob of the front door and the dead bolt. He reached and flicked the bolt over and made sure it was locked.

He crossed back toward the kitchen, then he turned the flame off and looked it over. He looked back toward the bathroom door and Drew, Drew tracking Will's every movement. Will turned the knob again on the range. He heard the gas then the click as it caught fire. He tried to blow it out, but it only made the flames dance and move. After a couple seconds of experimenting one way or another with the gas he had still not been able to turn off the flame.

He looked back toward the rear door, and he now saw the shape of one of the guards pass across the curtained window. Will turned and saw out front the other guard approaching, his shape seen across the diffuse curtains Will had parted earlier. Likely they were going house to house and now they had come to this one.

Will turned and looked on the flame again. It was pale and small no matter what he did to it. Turned it up or turned it all the way down, he still did not have what he was looking for. Knowing this, and knowing he was likely dead one way or another, he turned the range all the way down and put a hand on either side of the oven and pulled it out. The sound was loud and each inch he gained seemed to him like a shot fired or a flare launched high into the air that said, here I am.

When he got the oven far enough away from the wall he mounted the counter as quickly as he could and, getting his back to the wall above and his feet braced against the rear paneling of the oven, he pushed. The sound now was unavoidable. Loud as could be. He pushed as hard as he could possibly push and the oven went over and crashed across the floor. He could smell gas. And looking down he saw where the hose had come loose from the wall, and he could hear the hiss of it there in the room with him.

He came down off the counter and crossed to the back door. He saw the shape of the guard in the window and without pausing opened up the door and saw the guard swinging the barrel of his AR-15 machine gun up. Will grabbed it just as the man pulled the trigger, a series of bullets going into the wall just to the right of Will's hip and leg. Will felt the warm barrel in his hand, and he pulled the man forward into the house where he now fell across Drew's outstretched legs. Before the guard could turn or get the machine gun around, Will had already taken the .38 from his belt and he struck the man hard across the back of his head and watched his body flatten and go limp.

At the front door, the other guard was now trying the knob. Will could see the mechanism turning then the door rattling as he tried to get the door to open. Will fired one shot into the door at about head level. He heard the guard swear and dive into the gravel beyond, but Will did not think he'd hit him.

Will looked the first guard over, but decided there was no time to try and wrestle the strap of the AR-15 off his shoulder and from underneath his now-unconscious body. Instead, Will lifted Drew up and went out through the rear door of the house and into the open beyond. He had only begun to smell the gas, and now as he came into the open land outside the house he felt almost as if he wore it like a cape around his neck, dragging it forth upon the world.

He had replaced the .38 in the waist of his pants, and he ran with his two hands holding tight to Drew's legs, just behind the knees, while Drew bounced and moaned, riding on his belly across Will's shoulder. On his other shoulder Will still carried his rifle, and he ran with a labored gait from the back of one house to the next much the same way he had threaded his way among them earlier.

He could hear the siren now louder than it had sounded in the house. He made it nearly halfway to the church, when a spray of automatic gunfire tore up the earth beside his feet then thudded in a line across the wood of the nearest house. He did not even turn to look for who had fired on him before he cut and went through the passageway between two houses then came to a stop at the far edge.

Drew was heavier than Will had thought and he could not move as he had wanted to. He paused and looked around the gravel roadway at the members of Eden's Gate that had converged farther down, and he knew he could not run fast enough to get away. He was waiting on that house to blow and it felt like an eternity had passed. He wondered if somehow they had managed to stop the gas, or if they had found the Sterno behind the closed bathroom door.

Behind him, he saw now the shadows of three gunmen approaching the place where he'd cut and disappeared between the houses. The sun was behind them. He could see their shapes and he could see the long barrels they carried that were either machine guns or those of shotguns.

He watched their figures only long enough to understand that he could not be there when they arrived, and now, taking a quick look out on the gravel drive again, he sprinted as fast as possible out and up the road toward the church ahead. It was high ground and he knew if he could reach it and get his rifle from his shoulder he might have some advantage over those below who had been summoned by the siren and the sound of gunfire.

He reached the church just as he saw the three gunmen come around the corner and move after him up the road. Without even thinking about it he threw Drew to the ground as soon as they had cover. He came back around to the corner of the church and flicked the safety forward then leveled the rifle and took his shot. He shot the first man just above his chest. Will watched the bullet hit him in the right collarbone, and then he watched the blood mist and carry on the breeze as the bullet moved through him and exited somewhere past his shoulder blade. He was down in the gravel as soon as Will shucked the casing then pushed the bolt forward again, his eye looking down the scope.

He could hear the man's cry and he could hear the other men calling to him, but no one dared move to get him from where they'd dove themselves as soon as Will had fired. Down the gravel road Will could see many had hidden in among the houses. He watched the shadows of their movements and, as he ran the scope across the road, he watched a group of five break cover from one house, dashing for another. He shot at them, but he put the bullet low and watched it dig in among the dirt. The church members diving to the ground then scrambling up on hands and knees as they either went back the way they'd come or reached the protection of the next nearest house.

He shucked the bullet casing and loaded the chamber anew. Down in the road the man was crying for someone to come get him. He managed now to roll and get one arm beneath him, dragging himself across the road. The dirt and gravel beneath appeared slick and dark from the blood pouring from his back and front. Will shot at him again and watched him startle. The bullet had gone wide, but Will had placed it a foot in front of him, in the direction he had been going. The man was now too scared to move as he resigned himself to simply lying there, moaning and calling for his friends.

Will shucked the shell casing then, and as he loaded in another bullet, he saw first the shadow of the big man coming around the corner of the church, then the man himself. Will swung the Remington, but it was too late and the big man caught it in his hands and forced it back down upon Will. The rifle held crossways in his hands and the big man pressing the forestock now across Will's windpipe as both big man and Will went to the ground in a tumble.

Will tried to kick out, but his legs and knees landed in awkward places. The man was at least a half foot taller than Will and probably had fifty pounds on him. And as Will fought to free himself he could feel the man was muscle and sinew and not much else. With his hands Will tried to push the rifle up off his throat, but it was like trying to bench press several hundred pounds and the most he could get was a half inch before the man forced the rifle down again.

Will started to lose consciousness. He could see the black beginning to spot his vision. His mind swooned and then for a moment Will's sight went totally out, but he managed to overcome it. He pushed up on the rifle and felt the man rise a little. Will was left for a second to gasp at the air before the big man put his full weight down atop Will's throat again. The smell of the big man's breath in Will's face and the teeth of the man seen bared with the effort of keeping Will down against the ground.

Will could still hear the man in the road calling for his friends, but it was growing fainter now, and Will was not sure if that was because the man was bleeding out, or if it was that Will himself was about to die, suffocated with his own rifle.

When the big man arched his back up, calling out in pain, his face suddenly seen as a web of vein and muscle tissue, Will could only roll and cough, gasping now to get more oxygen within his lungs. The rifle was turned loose now from the man's hands and as Will rolled and tried to master himself, he watched the big man turn and saw his own hunting knife there in the man's lower back. Will turned his head and saw Mary May now stepping backwards as the big man swiveled, clawing for the knife.

He was going after Mary May now and he grasped for the knife and missed then grasped for it again. Finally, on his third try, he got his fingers on the hilt and pulled it from his own back, while at the same time making a sound Will had only heard a few times and never from a man. It was animal and tortured and in it Will heard the anger and the hatred building now into certain violence. Mary May backed up even more and the big man advanced upon her, Will's knife still within his hand.

When Will brought the rifle up and fired, the shot went straight, digging up through the man's back ribs and exiting through the heart. He fell over almost immediately, turning slightly as he went. And when he landed there was a stillness seen in the body suggesting he would never move again.

Mary May bent down and got the knife and came forward

toward Will. He could see the blood spatter on her face and on her clothes. Her collar was open almost all the way down her chest and Will saw how the blood ran from the fresh tattoo then disappeared in the cleavage formed by her bra. Will coughed and still he could not get the oxygen he needed. They were in rough shape, both of them.

Down on the road the man had stopped calling for his friends, but there was the sound now of footsteps making their way up toward them. Will bent and drew the .38 from his waist, then going to the corner of the church again, he fired twice, aiming the gun barrel down the small hill. He snuck his head out for a second and saw how his pursuers had scattered once again and soon were all back in hiding. Will simply looked on the place the man had been, and he saw that they had come and gotten him, and that he might be somewhere now getting the medical assistance he would need.

When Will looked back at Mary May she was waiting for him, kneeling over her brother and looking back at Will. Will stumbled over. He felt weak, but every breath he took seemed to give him new strength. As he moved toward her, he bent and picked up the rifle from the ground then loaded new cartridges from his pockets.

"Where's John?" Will asked. It was the first thing he said to her and he felt badly that it was not to ask how she was, but he knew they simply did not have the time. She was alive and keeping her that way was what now mattered most.

"Drugged," she said. "But I heard others back there and I know they're coming. The siren is even louder out on the road than it is back here."

Will looked past her to the stand of trees that surrounded the compound. He thought of the hundreds of tattoos he'd seen in that room. He had seen many people, but he had not seen hundreds. He spun and went to the corner of the church again and fired on the first thing he saw; a window in a house halfway down the road shattered then fell inward from its frame.

When he came back to Mary May he reached down and took the knife from off the ground where she had left it. He wiped the blood on his shirt then stuck it back down within his sheath. Next, he brought up the .38 and handed it over to her. "Three shots left," he said, watching her stand and then take one wobbly step toward him.

"Jerome is still waiting for us?" she asked. She turned slightly and looked in the direction of the far bluff.

"You can barely walk," Will said. "Can you make it?"

"I have to."

He looked her over. Her eyes were not tracking right and she was covered in her own blood and the blood of the man Will had shot. "You'll make it," Will said. He bent low to pick Drew up off the ground. Will used his legs and hefted Drew upward, feeling the man try and fight against the electrical cords that bound him, and which held the gag about his mouth. Paying little notice to Drew and still high on the adrenaline that had flooded his system, Will told Mary May to go as straight as she could and look for the big nurse log by the roadside. "Jerome will be there."

"Why tell me that?"

"Because you're going to need to find him and you're going to need to tell him how to find us." Will went to the corner of the church now and with Drew still over his shoulder he peaked out around the edge and several guns opened up on him immediately.

Will came cautiously back to where Mary May had flattened herself to the side of the church. "Go," Will said. "They've seen me and they've seen your brother. They don't know you're up here and they don't know which way you're going. Tell Jerome we'll be a mile down on the road as he heads toward the state highway."

She looked at him like she didn't think any of this was a good idea and Will knew she was right. It wasn't a good idea. But he knew, too, it was better than anything else they had.

"Go," he said.

MARY MAY WAS ALONE. SHE HAD COME AROUND THE BACK OF the church then gone into the trees, running in the direction Will had pointed her. But only about a hundred yards in, with the compound still clearly seen behind her through the tall pines, she began to hear shooting and the yelling of men and women. When she turned, locating first the edge of the compound, then running her eyes across the landscape, she saw the houses farther on. The front of the church was visible as well, with the steeple rising above, and it was there that she saw most of the Eden's Gate people gathered. And seeing them she dropped and lay in the grass that grew everywhere between the trees.

They were a hundred yards away and though Mary May did not know where they had come from, she could see a great many of them. A few trucks were there, when before there had been none. And many of the people who had arrived carried rifles and guns and were dressed in flak jackets, outfitted as if they meant to go to war.

She watched and saw several turn and move away from her in the direction Will had gone. Soon after she heard gunfire, then farther out the dissonant return of Will's rifle, quickly firing over and over again. For the fifth or sixth time, she thought to turn and go back toward him, but she knew there was little she might do.

She carried with her the .38 revolver, three shots left within the cylinder. She looked down at her father's gun. She knew if Will and Drew were to make it out of there and to the road that ran farther up along the bluff, she was going to need to make it first to Jerome. If

Will came out on that road and Jerome was not there, or Will even had to wait a minute, it would not take long for Eden's Gate to surround and quickly overpower him. Like her, Will's advantage only lasted as long as he kept moving. And if she didn't move—if she didn't run, and run now—Mary May, Will, Jerome, and possibly even her brother, Drew, were all as good as dead.

She started running, moving away from the lake in the way Will had told her to go. Any effect of the drug was gone now, either sweated from her system or expunged by her own adrenaline. She was nearly at the dense trees that climbed the bluff when the first bullet round hit the nearest trunk. She turned only briefly and saw the ten or so members of Eden's Gate advancing toward her, and who had no doubt seen her running straight on toward the bluff and the road above that she hoped to use for her escape.

By the time she came to the incline of the hill and started to climb, the bullets from six or seven guns were digging up the earth all around her and the trees were coming apart in a hail of wood chips and falling branches. But then in an instant all the gunfire and the sound of the bullets digging up the woods completely stopped, and for a half second, she thought the world had been sucked up and away into the vortex of some tornado that had rendered the world mute.

The light of the explosion hit her first, followed closely by the sound and Mary May turned to see the mushroom cloud expanding, and moving ever higher there above the Eden's Gate compound. She'd been scrambling up the hillside with her hands outstretched on the incline and her feet digging beneath her as she climbed. She looked back down the way she'd come and saw between the thin pines below a new column of smoke rising to the sky. She moved over until she could see what was left of a house. Just a dark black patch in the otherwise brown and green expanse below. Will had told her nothing of a house exploding and for longer than she should have, she stared at the place the house had been and wondered now whether Will and Drew in some way had been within.

She had little time to dwell on any of this. She could not explain what had happened and though she was worried, she had to believe Will and Drew had not doubled back somehow and made a final stand within the house. Looking now, she saw several of the church members had followed her into the forest and while they had turned, taking in this new disaster, Mary May cut across the slope, moving with the swiftness of some mountain animal. And now as she moved up she could see she'd increased her lead as the slope began to round.

The sun was still out, but it had begun to lower toward the horizon and the chill of the place could be felt now against her skin. The shirt John had ripped down the middle hung open and the exposed skin of her chest was covered in a collection of sweat, blood, ink, and the dirt of her own escape. Sometimes she moved fully upright, but mostly she had climbed with her hands outstretched, the gun wedged down the back of her pants as she went.

She chanced one more look back the way she'd come, letting her vision pan across the slope. Nothing could be seen but the wavering flow of wind as it moved through the branches above. No sound of rocks cut loose by those that followed her. No gunshots. No shouts or voices. The place seemed eerily normal to her, and it was this sense of normality among the more current chaos that frightened her most. She took one last look back across the path she'd made, then moved, hands outward on the slope again. All the while she thought that if she'd heard just one shot fired far out there in this landscape of forest and lakeshore, she might have felt some relief for Will or for her brother, but that she had not heard anything at all now scared her more than all that had come before.

· · ·

SHE CAME OVER THE TOP OF THE HILLSIDE WITH A CHILL SWEAT across her brow and down along her exposed clavicle. Through the trees she saw the road ahead. She pushed herself up and went into a full run. She was midway to the road when she saw Jerome. He was just south of where she'd thought he'd be, closer even than she'd hoped.

Jerome met her halfway and she fell against him and he held her for only a moment before turning her toward the ancient Oldsmobile. "Where's Will?" he asked. He looked now to the trees and forest she had herself run from. "He isn't with you?"

They reached the car and she let him help her with the door then help her to sit within. She was breathing hard and the sweat felt cool on her skin now in a way it hadn't before.

"What about Will? I heard the explosion. I came out to the edge of the hill but I couldn't see anything but smoke rising up above the trees. Is he okay?"

This was a hard question for her. She hadn't had time to process it, she hadn't had much more of a thought in her head than to simply escape. Run. Climb. Get the fuck out of there. But now, with Jerome waiting on her she did not know what to say. She looked back toward the forest. She almost wanted to see Will and her brother there. Will making his own escape, running, trying to find them where they sat. But no one was there. Just the wind through the trees—just the emptiness of the forest as it stared back at her. "I'm not sure Will made it," Mary May said, her eyes still on the forest.

"He's dead?"

"I don't know." She turned away from the forest. She looked to Jerome. She looked on the road ahead. "We need to go," she said. "We need to get out of here before we can't get out of here at all."

He looked at her, and then he closed the door. He came around the front of the car then pulled his own door open and sat in the driver's seat. He leaned forward and cranked the engine.

"I told Will to get my brother," Mary May said. "But we couldn't all get out together. Will and Drew went one way and I went the other. Will said they'd meet us down the road. But I'm just not sure if they made it." She could feel her voice beginning to break a little at the edges. This—being in Jerome's car—was the first time in nearly a day she had had a chance simply to sit and to reflect on her own existence. To realize how very, very dangerous Eden's Gate had become.

Jerome hit the gas and they started down the double track. She looked out on the road ahead then turned and looked back at the place where she'd come up over the hill. She wondered about her brother and she wondered about Will and whether either of them were still alive.

WILL HAD TOLD HER "Go" AND HE'D WATCHED MARY MAY TURN and run toward the stand of trees and that was the last he saw of her.

He held Drew up over his shoulder and the man's weight alone was almost enough to buckle Will at the knees. But he thought now, you got yourself into this, said you'd go get the brother like a fool. Now what?

He set out in a heavy trot, his boots scuffing across the dirt as he cut down toward the rolling lands just beyond the lake. He came off the small hill where the church sat and ran on into the lowlands, scraped by glacial flows a few thousand years before, but now populated by ferns and trees. Ahead, through the sparse growth of forest he saw where the hillside began, moving unevenly up toward the

high bluff and the road that ran atop it, the feel of the rifle swinging on the strap over his shoulder, the weight of Drew upon his
other side. No one shot at him or followed him and, still moving, he
turned slightly to the side and looked back at the church and Eden's
Gate and he wondered why.

The sound of the trucks froze him right there in place. He turned
fully now and looked back toward the compound. Five trucks were
rolling in past the gate, the dust moving off them as they went. And
as Will watched he knew without a doubt that everything he'd gone
through already that day had nothing on what was now approaching.

The trucks came up the drive, winding their way past the houses.
Will was a couple hundred yards from the church, standing in the
forested flatlands that came up from the lake, his view of the place
seen through stands of pine, but the pine trunks were not dense
enough to stop the trucks if they decided to turn and go for him.

Ahead, in the direction he needed to go, there was another quarter mile or so before he would reach the protection of the bluff. He
was exposed and though he had felt isolated and alone when he
had come down from the church and moved past the preliminary
makings of the perimeter fence, a feeling of desperate solitude now
seemed to emanate up from within his marrow.

Working quickly, Will dropped Drew to the ground then raised
the rifle and put the lens to his eye. He could see the trucks still
coming, they had almost reached the church. Many Eden's Gate
members were waiting there and as Will moved the rifle scope to
the people, Holly and a few others he recognized, he saw all of them
were pointing out across the compound and into the trees to the
place he now stood looking back.

He swung the rifle up then bent and grasped Drew and put him
back up over his shoulder. The man struggled for a moment but
Will simply set off across the lowlands as fast as he could go, jostling

Drew across his shoulder as he went. The first shot was heard as it buzzed past a few feet above his head. The next went wide and he saw it dig into a pine trunk to his left. Will cut and moved, veering across the land, trying to get as much forest between him and those who were shooting at him.

When he looked back he could see all five trucks had stopped right there next to the church and men had begun to move out and drop from the truck beds. He watched a distant rifle flare and he heard the shot. The bullet cut across the air a foot in front of him. They had a man like him up there, with a scope and hunting rifle, and Will knew now it was only a matter of time before a shot went true.

Will ran on. He dropped into a small depression between two rolling hills that held a dry creek at the bottom, and when he came back up the opposite rise and turned to look toward the church only two trucks were now parked there. Dust hung in the air and he knew almost without a doubt that the other three trucks were coming for him.

He gained the rise just as another bullet tore up the earth beside his foot, the dirt spraying high across his arm and side. He knew he was going to lose this one. He knew the bullets were getting closer. He came to the top of the rise and he went down the opposite side but he stopped and looked behind him. A bullet cut the air and Will dropped to the ground and with a shout from beneath the gag, Drew went rolling away from him and lay sideways down the hill, still struggling against the cording that wrapped his wrists and ankles.

Will could hear the trucks closing in on him, the sound of gravel and dirt echoing across the nearby lake and in among the trees. He kept his eyes forward. He had good cover here, but he knew it would not last if they caught him and surrounded him where he lay. Looking ahead he heard the engines working up the rise that stretched away from the compound. Then suddenly he saw them. They came into view moving as fast as possible, slowed only by the trees they had to weave among.

For a second all three of the trucks broke into the open, crossing a barren patch of meadow within the forest. Will watched them come. He was slightly above them and from time to time he lost them behind the trunks of pine and underbrush. The drivers navigated across the uneven ground and the engines raced as they came into the open and gunned their motors across the open meadow. From back atop the small hill where the church sat another rifle flare was seen. The bullet hit just before him, spraying dirt and bits of rock upward in the air.

He had no time. He had nothing but a sick feeling in his stomach that heralded the coming of his own destruction. Another bullet hit and sprayed him again with dirt. He looked to where the man was standing in the bed of one of the two remaining trucks by the church. He stood there with the rifle braced up over the roof of the cab and Will could see the glint of the scope there in the light of the lowering sun.

Will brought his own rifle around. He estimated there was now almost a quarter mile between this man and him. He looked at the way the nearby grass was moving, he looked at the trunks between him and the church. He measured the space between and the crosswind. He allowed for drop and even offered up a prayer. He put the scope to his eyes now and he thought if there is one thing you do right today, let this be it.

The rifle jumped and Will had time only to settle the scope back on his eye as he watched the man atop the truck buckle back and fall away.

Now the trucks had come across the little meadow and Will

watched them through the scope, the sound of the engines racing and the men in the passenger seats pointing on ahead and one now moving up and out of the open window, assault rifle in hand as the truck bore down on Will. Less than a thousand feet of space now to close.

Will worked the bolt. Then he took aim through the trunks of pines that made up the forest between him and them. He fired. He worked the bolt again. He kept firing from the prone position there atop the little rise and he watched the bullets spark and skip across the metal of hoods and siding. He watched the windshield crack and spider web on the nearest truck. He worked the bolt till there were no cartridges left to fire and the casings lay about him in the grass, hot from within the chamber.

The trucks were eating up the land, navigating both forest floor and the tree trunks that grew everywhere about. Will dug in his pockets and brought the last of his .308 cartridges up. Some fell and were lost there among the low vegetation, mixing in among the spent casings and blades of grass. He loaded and slammed the bolt forward, and he was firing again, rapidly, working through the cartridges as fast as they would fire.

He took the mirror from one truck, flattened out one tire and watched the driver fight to keep control, the truck soon sliding and going over, rolling down an incline and then out of sight. Will shot and fired again, the bullet digging through the engine block of another truck, and the truck now puttering to a stop. Will was firing even as the men dove and moved for cover. He was near out of bullets by the time the third truck had come within a hundred yards. Will stood now and ran, knowing if he did not move they would soon be on him.

He reached Drew and, with the adrenaline still coursing, Will brought Drew up over his shoulder and he pumped up the rise beyond with his thighs feeling like they had caught on fire. It was then, almost as the truck was on them, that the little house blew, the light seen in the forest boughs, and the sound following soon after.

Will turned. He had thought that the house would not go. He had thought that if it was to go that the gas would have ignited already. And that the little house was not there and the cloud of fire and smoke now rose above it all was to him almost as much of a shock as he could now see it was to those back at Eden's Gate and to the remaining men who followed him in the truck.

The last truck veered. He watched the driver shift and look behind as if the fireball might be heading out across the land to get them. Will paused only for a second, recognizing this was the time he needed to make the bluff and the dense trees and forest that clung to the rocks there.

He took off running again. His feet feeling like two pieces of stone pulled along behind his body. His heart felt inside his chest like it was pumping something that was half acid through his bloodstream. And though he had been cutting a fairly straight path before, he moved down from atop the nearest rise and went running in the depression, keeping hidden from the truck behind, following the curve between the two rises that he could see now would lead him directly to the bluff.

He reached the bluff in the same moment the truck came blaring over the edge of the rise, the engine heard slipping down through the gears as the driver pulled the wheel around. Tires and engine ate up the same tracks Will had left only moments before as he had cut his own path across the sparse forest floor. Drew grunted with each step as Will labored toward the steep incline of the bluff, the truck coming on fast, running over the thin underbrush that grew everywhere beneath the trees.

The gunman in the passenger seat now leaned out and began

firing a submachine gun from the window. The bullets raking through the trees. Will slipped then righted himself, one hand holding tight to Drew's legs and the other held out against the hillside. He was trying now to move upwards on the slope, and he fell beneath his weight and that of Drew's. He slipped nearly five feet before he could get his toes dug in somewhere and then reach and try to stop Drew who had come rolling after him.

Now Will turned and brought the rifle around. He saw the truck pull sideways down below, the gunman in the passenger seat still. Will put the scope on him and fired. The shot caught the man in the right bicep. He spun a bit with the force then fell out of the door, scrambling now to get around the back of the bed and find some cover.

Both driver and passenger wore flak jackets and Will sighted what he could, seeing how each had taken up a place behind the body of the truck. He had only one cartridge left and he levered it down within the chamber. He was exposed there on the hillside. He had wedged his heels into the loose soil and dried pine needles that lay everywhere beneath the trees, and he braced his back against Drew.

When the submachine gun came up over the body of the truck and fired wildly into the trees and shrubs about them, Will watched through the scope, waiting as the man came into view. Will fired just as the man turned to run for the trees and the slope on which he sat. The bullet entered the side of the man's ribs, just between the two plates within the vest. The man went down immediately and the gun lay a foot ahead of him in the grass, but he did not move to get it and as Will put the scope across him, he could see the man's unmoving eyes.

There were no bullets left and Will gave the truck and the driver who hid behind it one last look before he moved and brought Drew to his feet. Drew stood awkwardly on the slope. Now, weak as he was from carrying Drew this far, Will used that same slope to get a little below Drew and placed his shoulder into Drew's stomach and bent and lifted. He felt his muscles fighting to keep their hold as he went up the hill again, hoping for both their sakes that Mary May had made it to Jerome.

He was almost at the top of the bluff when he looked behind and saw the driver now climbing upward through the trees. The driver, like all the rest, wore a protective vest and Will could see the butt of a shotgun where it emerged above his shoulder. The gun bobbing along behind him as he climbed.

Will had nothing left. He looked ahead of him through the trees. A low spine of rock ran atop the bluff and beyond. Looking past the smooth surface of rock—seen between shrubs and trees—there were patches of dirt and gravel Will thought might be the road. He moved on, his own heart and the scuff of his boots across the ground the only thing to hear. He was running on empty and he knew it. No sweat now felt across his skin and a desperate need felt in the bowels of his stomach and on his tongue for liquid. Each footfall he took feeling like it would be his last.

He came to the top of the rock. He could see now the double track of the road about fifty feet on, down a little gully and across an opening in the trees. Will looked behind him. The driver could not be seen and the idea now of even trying to bring Drew down the gully to where the road sat below was like trying to convince him to climb Everest without rope or oxygen of any kind.

Will slumped and brought his knees down upon the earth. He levered Drew off onto the ground and now he straightened. The effort of carrying Drew through the forest and up the bluff felt as if it had compounded and fused each of Will's vertebrae into a rigid growth of bone. Not wanting to ever lift the man again, Will met

Drew's waiting eyes then put a foot out and sent the man rolling down the incline toward the road and the bottom of the gully where Will could see in wetter months a stream would flow.

Will was up again just as he saw the driver come through the trees a couple hundred feet behind. Without another thought, Will went over the side and down, sending bits of rock and pebble out ahead of him as he went. At the bottom, he wrestled the gun from his shoulder then scrambled upward toward a gnarled growth of tree roots that had come exposed at one point from the soil. Climbing up, he wedged himself as far under the grip of these roots as possible. With the rifle off his shoulder and no bullets to load it with, Will now took the hunting knife from his belt. He held it in his hand and looked down toward the bottom of the gully where Drew lay watching him.

There was a sound now of the driver coming through the trees. Will heard how his steps changed as he moved from the forest floor onto the smoothness of the rock. Will leaned out a little. He could see the man move cautiously to the edge of rock, the shotgun now held before him as his eyes caught sight of Drew there at the bottom of the incline. The driver came over the edge and down the incline, moving toward Drew.

Will waited as long as he could. The man was no more than ten feet from him now. With knife in one hand and bits of gravel and dirt held within the other palm, Will stood from his hiding place. Drew's eyes were open wide, looking past the driver to Will, and by the time the driver caught wind of what was happening and turned Will had already thrown the dirt, blinding the driver then shoving the knife upward through his neck.

They went to the ground together. The driver making the small dying sounds that Will had come to know so well when he'd been twenty years of age and in another country far across the world.

Blood welled from the windpipe of the man and the gurgle of breath could be heard as the driver struggled to fill his lungs. Will had heard this sound both from men he'd killed, and from friends who had lain dying in his arms, and he had liked it then no more than he did now.

All he'd done that day could not be changed and he felt helpless. People had died because of him, and at his hand, and though he knew it had been them or him, he could in some way still not accept it. He had thought all of this long behind him.

It came rushing at him now. Who he'd been in war and after, when he'd come home. Who he was now—who time and regret had made him. The deaths of his wife and daughter felt to him like a wound that would never close. The man he'd become because of them. The part he'd played in all of this. He couldn't look away anymore. He couldn't just hide and hope it all went away. He knew he was doing something now. He hoped it was enough for absolution. He hoped somehow that this was what he needed to do to earn his forgiveness from God, or from whatever being out there decided his fate one way or another. He had caused so much pain and done so little to redeem himself. He hoped this was enough.

He looked over at Drew, who was watching him in all this. In all of Will's raw anguish. The thoughts going around in Will's head that seemed to have exploded from out of the depths of his mind and then seeped like oil through every crevice. He wondered if he was losing it. He was so tired. So very tired and once more he felt something move inside of him and come loose and he coughed it up and stood looking at it on the ground, a clot of blood that was the size and shape of a golf ball. An ulcer surely grown in his stomach— a physical manifestation of his own fears and doubts concerning Eden's Gate.

He looked at Drew again. The man's eyes fixed on him, a look of disgust across his face. Will's head swam and he nearly fainted except he knew he couldn't. It was only the sound of car tires now that kept him from passing out. Then, from somewhere down the road, he heard the racing of an engine. He took the shotgun from the man who now was dead and Will lay there with the stock braced across the man's chest and the barrel pointed down the road. He had little will to move and he waited now to see who would come, knowing he would fight if it came down to it, that he would use each and every shell.

IV

I walk among the people as the true prophet. And I spread the word to all that would follow and heed the warnings put in place by the false gods we call government. For I am the messenger and to each that I spread my hand in friendship—to each who is willing—to each who would embrace our family and bring us unto their heart, let it be known that they, too, are us. They too are our messengers and they too have our love. And in this way, we will be united, for everywhere we go we will be among followers of Eden's Gate. In every walk of life, in every class, in every home—be that home in field, forest, or town—we will find brothers and sisters of like mind, for we are them and they are us.

—THE FATHER, EDEN'S GATE
Hope County, Montana

WHEN WILL WOKE THE SKY WAS A PALE BLUE LIKE THAT seen only within three or four nights of the fullest moon. He had fallen asleep with his head resting against the rear passenger window of the Oldsmobile. He sat up and felt every one of his muscles unhinge like some old rusted bit of metal long forgotten by the light of day. He saw he was alone but for Mary May who, like him, lay with her head against the front passenger window. Jerome was missing from the driver's seat and so, too, was Drew.

Will looked around now and found at his feet the flak jacket and the shotgun he had taken off the dead man and brought with him into the car. His rifle sat up front with Mary May and he leaned now and looked to where it rested across her knees. There was a dread rising in him that he was alone, that Jerome or Drew might now be taken and Mary May in her unmoving slumber might actually be very dead.

With one hand Will brought a finger across her neck and pressed it to the skin. The warmth he felt was immediate, and there beneath his fingers was the pulsing of the blood within the vein. He brought his hand back and looked out into the blue night. Fields stretched out for some length and the farmhouses among them, some with no lights to see, but others glowing faintly from behind the soft curtain of a window.

He cracked the door and took with him the shotgun then carefully closed the door again and stood upon the grass margin of a dirt road. Jerome had parked the car atop a dike. Will could see to either side the flatness of the fields and the way the moon fell across the land, leaving little left in shadow.

When Will went to the edge of the dike and looked over, he saw how the slope ran away from him to a stream below. The water rolling past in that glimmer of light was itself a reflection of the sky above that he could see would change nightly based upon the weather and the fullness of the moon. He ran his eyes out and saw where Jerome was standing another hundred or so feet upstream, while to his right, down in the vegetation sat Drew.

Will could hear nothing of what they said but he could see them both staring off across the river at a group of four horses there across the way. Will moved down the road then stopped and gave a last look to the Oldsmobile there before heading down the slope toward the water below. When he came within five feet of them they turned and followed his movements until he stood beside Jerome.

"Beautiful creatures," Jerome said. His eyes were on the horses across the stream. The animals standing four abreast with their heads held outward over the wire fencing. Each bending from time to time to eat from the tall shoots of grass that had been cultivated to gigantic proportion from the water there.

Will looked at the horses, then he looked to Jerome. He bent and leaned out and took in Drew where he sat with his hands still tied behind his back, but, as Will saw now, no cord around his mouth or even around his ankles. "You're taking chances with him you shouldn't take," Will said.

"He worshipped once in my church and I have not forgotten that."

"Yeah, well I wouldn't be so sure he remembers it the way you do," Will said. He ran a hand down his cheek and felt the gouges left there by Drew's nails. "You really should be careful."

Jerome flashed the chrome .38 he carried in his off hand then looked to Drew and back to Will. "It's not hard to forget what we're dealing with. Especially with the way this one talks."

"He's been giving you the gospel?"

"They always seem to," Jerome said. "It's like they never read another book or heard another voice than that of The Father or that book of his he calls his bible. They all hide behind it, even Drew."

"And you?"

"Me?"

"How is your religion any different?"

"I'm not forcing it on anyone," Jerome said. "I'm here as an interpreter. And sometimes, even to me, the Bible is a foreign text. I'm not the end-all. I'm nothing like that and neither is God. You've got to do what you've got to do, whether God is with you or whether God is not. I don't make excuses otherwise."

"Sounds like you've been down here having some discussion."

"I wouldn't call it that."

"What would you call it then?"

"I'd say we're at an impasse."

Will ran his eyes over Drew. He was watching the horses but Will could tell he was listening, too. "What's he say?" Will asked Jerome.

"He says there's nowhere we can go that Eden's Gate can't follow us, and he says wherever we go, and to whoever we find that might help us, their lives are forfeit. He says John will burn buildings to the ground."

"John is pleasant that way, isn't he?"

Jerome was watching the horses, but he turned now and looked at Will. "We can't take him or Mary May to my church, or to the bar. Both places would be too easy."

"I know it," Will said. "I don't think the cabin they gave me would be any better. I think going back to town is out, too. There are too many eyes there watching."

"Mary May needs medical attention. We need somewhere to go that she can wash and clean the tattoo John gave her." Jerome looked to Will. "You need medical attention, too. Drew said you're sick. He said we shouldn't put stock in you, that you're a dead man walking. He said you coughed up blood and nearly passed out right there in front of him. Is that true?"

"I'll be fine."

"That doesn't sound fine to me," Jerome said.

"I'm a healer. I just need time and I just need space. We need to get out of here and we need to do it now," Will said.

"I don't know what to do. Drew says that Eden's Gate is always watching. And I don't see any reason to think otherwise."

"No, I don't either." Will looked out on the fields and the houses farther on. He didn't doubt that even now someone was probably watching. He took a few steps then put a knee down in the grass and placed the shotgun there beside him. He scooped water from the stream and brought it to his face. He washed his cheeks and neck. He dipped his forearm in the water and felt the coolness of the liquid across the broken skin.

He was still thirsty but he knew he had water in his bag. He stood now and looked to Drew. Something about the whole thing was bothering him. Will thought about Lonny. He thought about the surety the man had right up until he went over the edge. Will picked the shotgun up and walked to where Drew sat. He put the barrel to the man's chest. "You know something we don't?" Will asked.

"They're going to burn you, Will. They're going to gut you and string you up with your own intestines and they're going to burn you when they're done."

"You're an asshole, Drew."

Drew tried to spit on him but the spittle missed and fell harmlessly to the grass.

"Asshole," Will said again, stating it like the fact it was. "You notice they didn't seem to care that when they shot at me, they also shot at you? You should probably think about that."

"John is going to find you," Drew said. "He's not going to be nice, either. You're one of us, Will. You'll always be one of us and there are punishments for those that go against us, for those that accepted The Father and then looked away."

"I don't doubt it," Will said. "But right now we need to clear something up before we get into whatever cluster fuck you seem to think is coming." He pushed the barrel harder into Drew's chest and Drew went to the ground. Will now handed the shotgun over to Jerome and told the pastor to hold it on Drew while Will checked him.

Will ran his hands up one leg then down the other. He patted Drew down across both arms, his chest, his back, and every place Will could think to check. When he was done he stood and stared down at the man and shook his head. "I think he might just be plain crazy," Will said, taking the shotgun back from Jerome.

"What did you think you'd find?"

"A transponder. John was using them in the mountains. He says his eldest brother Jacob uses them to track wolves. I found out the hard way that they also use them to track people."

"But you didn't find one?"

"No. I would have thought he'd have one the way he's talking now."

"Then we're okay?" Jerome asked.

"I guess so. But it still doesn't solve our current problem."

"Where to go?"

"Yes," Will said.

"You got nothing?"

"I got something," Will said. "There's a little food there, and medical supplies. But it's not ideal. It's someplace I've been avoiding for a long time now. But it might be the best we have."

SHE WAS AWAKE WHEN THEY STOPPED BEFORE THE GATE. SHE looked out on the hillside. The driveway went on for another hundred yards or so and at the top of the hill she could see the low roof of the house and the dark windows that looked across the property and down over the land beyond.

"I remember this," Mary May said.

Will leaned forward from the backseat. "Your dad brought you and Drew here once or twice when you were really young and your mom was working at the bar. We used to barbeque a little and you and Drew would roll down the hill here. But that was a long time ago—twenty years or more."

She could see it held something still for him. She could see why he hadn't wanted to come here, but he had. For Will there was more locked away in this place than just rooms. "We'll be safe here?" she asked.

He looked again on the property. She saw his eyes swim a little in their sockets. The house atop the hill, with its view out across the county road below and the varied patchwork of farmland they could see farther on. "It's a good place," he said. "You all see how it backs up to the cliff there and makes it approachable from only one direction." She watched him look around again, watched his eyes land on the gate and the chain there with the padlock. "It will be good," he said again. "If they come, we'll see them before they're knocking on the doorway."

Jerome looked around at Will then back out on the gate. "You have a key for that padlock?" he asked.

Will shook his head. "Any claim I ever had on this place has long been lost to me. But we won't need it. I think you've taken us far enough," Will said. "We can't ask you for anymore. They don't know you're with us at this point and I was thinking it might be better for you if we kept it that way."

"You're asking me to leave you here?"

"I'm saying you should keep yourself safe."

"No," Jerome said. "That's not how we're playing this. In the next few days you're going to need things: food, water, supplies. That sort of thing. I can do that. We're going to hole up here and after everything dies down a bit I'm going to get the three of you out of here and we're going to go for help."

Mary May looked over at him. "What kind of help?"

"The sheriff would be a start."

"No," Mary May said. "I think he means well. I really do. I was there just a few days ago. I asked for his help. I told him what I would do. That I was going to go up to Eden's Gate to get Drew. I didn't talk to anyone else but him. You get it?"

"I think I see where this is going," Will said.

She turned and looked to Will then to her brother. "John was waiting for me. It was like he knew. He even said he knew why I was going up there," Mary May said. "I don't think it was the sheriff but someone told John I was coming. I just couldn't say who."

She watched Drew shrug. He turned and looked out the window. She wanted to say something more but she could see it would do no good.

The engine was still running and now Jerome reversed the car then brought it down off the drive into a little stand of trees that sat to the side of the gate. "I'm coming with you," he said, cutting the engine now and taking the keys from the ignition. "When this is done we'll get out of the county and look for some federal help. I've seen enough already to know this place needs it."

WITH HIS HUNTING KNIFE WILL CUT SLENDER BOUGHS FROM the trees then laid them atop the Oldsmobile. Stepping back he turned and looked the car over. He spoke with Jerome, "It's the best camouflage I can give."

"You'd have to be right up on it to know there was a car here," Jerome said. He looked around him now, looking to Mary May as if for a second opinion.

Mary May looked from the car to the gate. "Do you have bolt cutters in the house?"

Will ran his eyes to the house again. He'd looked up a hundred times at it already, as if he feared it would go away. "I'm not sure what's up there anymore. We'll see. There used to be some supplies put away, but I honestly don't know anymore. I'll look for a bolt cutter then come back down and cut the lock. Then we can bring the car up away from the road here."

"Just shoot it off," Drew said.

Will spun to look at the man. Will had in some way forgotten he'd been with them, staying quiet there on the ground where they'd put him after they took everything from within the car. Will shook his head now. "That seems a sure enough way to get your buddies looking out this way."

"They're your buddies, too," Drew said.

Will ignored him. He bent and picked up the backpack with his water, snares, traps, and remaining .308 cartridges within. He brought it to the gate and tossed it over. Next he slid the rifle in between the metal gate rails, making sure it was out of anyone's way.

Now, he told them to start climbing. They took with them the flak jacket and the shotgun. Jerome helped Mary May to get up and over the gate. Will and Jerome both noticed how hard it seemed for her to move her arms, each pull of muscle or stretch of skin causing her face to change. From what they'd seen of the tattoo they both knew why, in many places, the letters looked carved upon the bone.

Now, Will bent and lifted Drew up then brought him to the gate. And between the three of them they got him over. Will followed. He looked up at the house again. However it came out in the end, he knew without a doubt that this was where it had all started for him, one way or another, years before.

He was trying to hide what it meant for him to come back here, but he knew in some ways they must have known. He lifted his rifle and bag then turned back to the group and told them it was time to go. They walked two by two up the hill and though Will hoped to find some salvation here, he did not know what they would find, and though he had forgotten about this place for years, he wondered now if that had been true for all.

When they came to the top he could see the rope swing was still there beneath the lone tree like it had been when he'd given the property over. He stopped and stared at the two lengths of rope and the wooden seat below. He knew he was here for a reason, but he wondered now why the fear of death had been the deciding factor in his return. He stared at the swing while the others passed him by. When he was able to break free from the spell it had cast upon him, he turned and saw that Mary May, Jerome, and even Drew, were waiting on him, staring back at him from where they stood next to the house.

"Just taking a trip down memory lane," Will said. He had said it as a joke but no one laughed and they were all still watching him as he walked up. The single-story house had been left pretty much the same. The paint was chipping and the surrounding land was overgrown. In several places weeds grew out of the gutters, but it was his home still, even now that it wasn't.

He'd raised his daughter, Cali, here. He'd put that swing up himself, pushed her in it when she'd been little, watched her play on it when she got older. He looked on it now as if it had no reason to be here, though he knew very well that it did. He gave a piece of himself away when he gave this property to the church, and foolishly he thought he'd be rid of it.

Under a stone near the door he found the key. After turning the key in the lock he used his shoulder to push the door the rest of the way. The sound of the wood working against the frame was harsh in the relative silence. Shadows were waiting inside and warm trapped-away air ran out and met them where they stood. The air smelling of old locked-away places and the damp unused hint of dirt and mold.

He stepped in and ran his eyes about the room then took several steps inside, kicking an old beer can that sat there on the floor. He had not seen it and he heard it roll away from him then saw it move into the light of the moon that lay in a square on the living room floor.

"Looks like you had squatters," Jerome said. He had come into the room leading Drew behind him, Mary May last. She closed the door now and all of them looked about the place.

Will had never thought his drinking was as bad as it was until the morning after he had lost them. Even now, looking around, he could see how wrong he'd been about even that—his drinking had been even worse than he had thought. Empty bottles were everywhere, some from before the death of his wife and child, but many more were from after. He would drink them and toss them and, in one corner of the living room, a pile of shattered glass lay from all the bottles he had thrown. In spray paint on the wall above the broken glass was written the single word, MURDERER. Though Will knew they were all thinking it must have been someone else, Will knew he had written it with his own hand, and that he had meant it at the time.

He wished now that he'd died instead of them. He wished now that he had just pickled himself in alcohol, like he'd tried to do so many days and nights after they'd gone. And though it hurt him to think on it now, he wished they hadn't loved him as much as they did. Then, he thought, they wouldn't have been out on that road that night. But even as he thought it he knew it was not the answer. And if he was being truly honest with himself he knew he should have been the one to change.

"There should be some kerosene lanterns in the kitchen," Will said now. He looked around on the three of them. He could see the careful study they were giving this place, as if they'd stepped unwelcome into the prison of memories Will had made here. "Top shelf on the right. Matches should be there, too. And if the fuel is gone I think there is some more beneath the sink. At least there should be."

They went out of the room and he heard them rummage around, then find the lamps. First one went on then the other, he saw the warm glow build back in there and he heard their talk. There were cans of food and at the bottom of one shelf they found a twelve pack of soda water.

Will came into the kitchen and saw them laying out the plunder and already he could see that the simple fact of food had put them in a better mood. He tested the faucet but nothing came. Then he tested the stove and there was not a click or spark of any kind. He stepped away and stood trying to figure out what could be done.

After five minutes, he came back in with the old two-burner camp stove he'd used when he was a young man, freshly back from the war. He found fuel for it as well and after dialing up the fuel pressure, he tried the knob then heard the hiss of gas. With a match, he lit the burner and they all stood there in a bit of wonder while it danced then settled.

By the time Will had found the medical kit they had started heating green beans and corn in an ancient pan, and on the other burner they had concocted a kind of soup with diced spam and tomato paste, made fluid with water taken from cans of soda.

"It smells like heaven," Mary May said. She held the medical kit. "Thank you. I know that it must have been hard to come here."

"Twelve years is a long time," Will said. "I should be okay."

"But you aren't," she said. "We can see that and that's okay, too."

He looked at her. He had been trying not to meet her eyes. She had lost her mother and her father and maybe even her brother in the span of three weeks and she was the stronger one. He knew that. He could see it just as easily as she could probably see his own pain.

"My brother," she said, turning now to where Drew was slumped against one wall of the kitchen, his hands still tied behind him and his legs outspread on the kitchen floor. "I want to untie him. His fingers look blue at the ends. I know he's hurting." She had turned back to Will and he watched her and thought about what she was asking him to do.

Will went over to Drew then dropped down on his haunches and looked the man over. "Your sister says your hands are tied too tight, that true?"

"You can look at them yourself," Drew said. He had turned slightly, his eyes cast down to where his arms disappeared behind his back, as if they might share this moment somehow. "I can't feel anything past the wrists."

Will looked at the fingers. What Mary May had told Will was true. They looked a little gray in that light. Will bent and pulled them out so that he could better see them. Now, he looked away, running his vision to Mary May first, then to Jerome.

Jerome was standing at the two-burner stove, stirring the tomato soup. When Will's eyes went to him, the man—slowly and deliberately—shook his head in silent opposition to giving this man any freedom to hurt them.

Will stood now. He went back through the house. When he came back into the kitchen he held a length of climbing rope and some zip ties and a woman's shirt. He set these on the table just on the other side of the two-burner stove. Jerome was still looking at him, still watching, not saying anything.

Will dragged one of the chairs from the table and set it there in the center of the room. He looked to Mary May. "I know you love him. I know you want to help him. I want to help him, too. It's why he's here and not dead back there at Eden's Gate. But I also need to tell you that he can't be trusted. He might be family. He might be all you have left, but right now, in this situation, we really can't treat him that way."

She looked her brother over then looked back at Will. "Then what?"

Will walked to where the second kerosene lamp sat by the sink. He lifted it up and then, moving back toward her, he picked a can of soda from out of the twelve pack and delivered both to Mary May. "I'm going to untie your brother, but I want you to take that shirt and the supplies and go back there to the bathroom. Start to clean up that tattoo John gave you. I'm going to put Drew in this chair and tie his feet, then his chest, and then I'll cut his hands free."

"And you don't want me to help?" she asked.

"No," Will said. "I don't want you to help because if Drew gets loose at any time I don't want you stopping me. Or stopping Jerome. We mean to keep him safe but neither of us trust him. You understand?"

"I'm on your side," she said. "I could help." She looked past him to Drew and Will turned to see Drew watching all of this with amusement.

"I know that," Will said. "But things change quickly. It's why John sent Drew away when he started tattooing you. And it's why I'm sending you away now. Family makes people do strange things. That's all."

She looked around at all three of them, then she agreed. They watched her go down the hallway to the bathroom. The light from the lamp, refracted off the walls of the hallway, was the only thing to follow after she had gone. Then, far down, Will heard the sound of the bathroom door closing and afterwards there was no light to be seen at all.

Will brought Drew to his feet then walked him to the chair and set him down again. Jerome had already taken up the shotgun and angled off to the right for a clear shot that would not hit Will if Drew did decide to fight them. Will cut a length of rope away then tied it around the back of the chair, securing it in among the wood. Then he tied Drew's arms down at the elbows, looped the rope across his chest, and tied it all taut behind. He did the same to his ankles, looping the separate length of rope about the chair legs before securing each ankle to each chair leg. Only afterwards did Will cut the electrical cord from about Drew's wrists. The rope around his chest and arms was loose enough that he could, with difficulty, bring his arms around and set them on either thigh.

Will tested each rope then stepped back. He looked to Jerome then motioned for Jerome to lower the shotgun.

Drew sat there working his hands open and closed, repeating it over and over again. He looked straight at Will and smiled. "See, you can trust me," he said.

Will turned away. He found several thick blankets and some nails then tacked the blankets up across the front windows to block what light came from the lamp and the cooking. He was nearly done with this when he looked out the front window on the tree there and the swing moving slightly in the night breeze that came up the hill.

He let that vision pour into him for a time, memories in his head and the knot they created in his throat and in the muscles of his stomach. Then, in only a whisper, he said, "I hope wherever the two of you are you've made a life of it better than I ever could." He let that hang in the air for a while, then he reached up and hammered in the last nail.

IN THE MEDICAL KIT SHE FOUND GAUZE AND ALCOHOL. SHE found things like scissors and bandages, an ACE wrap, and the little metal clips that went along with it. She laid this all out before her on the bathroom counter. The light of the lamp flickering ever so in the stillness of the bathroom, causing each of the items and even the medical kit itself to wax and wane in shadow on the bathroom wall.

She listened for a time but she heard no struggle and she assumed everything had gone okay and even now her brother sat on the chair, his hands free. Mary May did not blame Will for the way he'd talked to her. She knew it was true, she knew when it came down to family, people did irrational things.

"Like crash their pickup truck and run into the mountains for a day or two," the woman in the mirror said to her, looking at her out of the lamplit gloom.

"John did try to give you an out," she said to herself. "He tried to tell you not to go up that mountain but then you did anyway and now you have this to deal with for the rest of your life." She pried one edge of her shirt down and away from her skin. It was stuck in places from either the blood or sweat that had dried there. She looked the word over. It was barely even visible with all the dirt and dust she had on her, and that stuck on her as if she was some fool from yesteryear who had let themselves be tarred and feathered.

She picked up the scissors now and cut the shirt all the way down then shucked it from off her shoulders and let it fall to the ground. She found the can of soda water Will had given her. She cracked the top, poured a little over some of the gauze, and began to wipe it down her chest. She followed the edges of the letters, not wanting to directly touch them yet, the skin beneath the dirt and blood looking red and swollen.

When she was done she brought out a separate swath of gauze, poured alcohol over it and then started in again, wincing with the pain, sometimes crying out as the alcohol touched the raw skin. When she was done she stood unmoving at the mirror, looking at the word there in the lamplight. The tattoo was dark on the skin, she could see in some places how John had gone over it several times, and then in other places she saw how he had used a lighter touch. The effect gave the tattoo a loose and somewhat lopsided appearance, like the drawings of a child.

ENVY. She closed her eyes, hoping in some way it would not be there when she opened them again. But it was there, spanning the skin between her collarbone and the beginnings of her bra, marking her. She thought about what John had said to her as he had put the sin across her chest. She knew she would not forget, but she knew, too, that the way she thought about it and the way John had intended it were two completely different things. She would not forget, and if John had killed her daddy, Mary May was certain she would come for John first.

She slipped one bra strap off, then the other. She kept the back clasped and began to press clean bandages down across the red and swollen skin. If she had lotion or some sort of ointment she would have used it, but everything she turned up was old and had separated within the bottle and certainly could not be trusted. Next, she wrapped the ACE bandage and secured it with the clips. It looked all right. Not professionally done but it worked for what it was.

She put the straps of the bra back over her shoulders then picked up the shirt Will had given her. She put the still-folded garment to her nose. Dust and locked-away places. Mildew, and the faint smell of another woman's perfume. It was his wife's and she'd known that since he'd brought it out to her. Now, Mary May let it fall full before her. A gray button-up blouse. She knew he'd picked it out because it would not sit atop the tattoo, but still it was not like the T-shirts she was accustomed to. She put it on and turned and looked herself over. It was almost as if she were someone else. It was almost as if it hadn't happened, but she knew no shirt could erase the tattoo from her mind, it would always be with her, however she chose to try and hide it.

When she opened the door and came out with the lamp held before her, she could smell the cooking. There was the sound of metal silverware and the low talking of the men. She walked forward but then stopped. In the living room the windows had all been covered with thick blankets, but the lightest of them showed a slight red flicker, like light seen on the bottom of a pool, diffuse and distant. She knew though that this was not light on the bottom of a pool, or anything as pleasant as that.

By the time she reached the window she was sure of it, something was burning. There was a faint smell in the air that had not been there before, rubber or something acrylic. She now had the blanket in hand and she parted it from the window and looked out. The fire lit the night up and the smoke rolled and billowed black into the sky, the flames licking upwards at a height of twenty or thirty feet. All of this was down at the edge of the property. Something had been set afire there at the gate, the flames rising and spreading upward into the trees overhead.

IT WAS JEROME'S CAR. WILL PUT THE SCOPE ON IT AND WATCHED the flames licking upward to the trees above. Many of the branches were now aflame and the thermals were working upward among the tree boughs and causing them to curl inward and dance in cruel fashion, like the last dying moments of some spider clutching at the air in spasm.

Will dropped the scope and moved back from the window. He had seen nothing but the car afire, windows no more than red flame and the dark exterior of the car burned an ashen gray beneath the moon. He had seen no one, but it did not mean they were not out there — they were. If the tattooed skins stapled to the walls had been any indication, it was likely John was there and many, many more.

When Will turned now, they were all waiting on him. Mary May right next to him, Jerome halfway across the room, and even Drew back there in the kitchen, still tied to his chair. "Get your shit," Will said to all of them.

He watched them staring back at him, seeing in them his own baffled expression. They had thought themselves safe. They had thought themselves free in that moment, but they had not been, and never had been, and it was Drew all the while who had been right. Eden's Gate would come for them and there was nowhere they could hide.

"Come on," Will said. "We need to go. There's no time left." He moved to where he'd dropped his bag. He brought out the box of rifle cartridges and emptied the contents into his pockets then stood, bringing the bag up with him. He was back at the window in another second. He put the scope out there on the night again, and he had to still the rattle of his nerves that now ran through him like a freight train.

Out there in the night, seen through the scope, was a mass of twenty or thirty people. All armed, all moving up the hill, fanning out around the property from one side to the other. And leading them was John. His dark shape and the dark shapes of those behind all lit by the rising flames, each among them like the Devil's own hellspawn set forth upon the world, walking ever nearer.

Will turned again and caught sight of Mary May, she was at the other window looking out, watching as Eden's Gate approached. She had stuck the .38 down the front of her waistband. She let the blanket drop and Will met her halfway across the room and together they found Jerome in the kitchen, standing over Drew with an old kitchen knife held in one hand.

"What should I do?" Jerome asked. "Should I cut him loose? We need to run. We already might be trapped."

Will looked to Jerome, looked at the knife then turned and looked back at the diffuse light of flame seen everywhere now at the windows, as if the whole of the property were on fire and not just the stand of trees there at the bottom of the drive. "We could let him go," Will said. "We should. There's a way to get out of here, but we couldn't carry him and we couldn't trust him to move as fast as we need to go." He turned back to them now. He looked from face to face, he could see the fear in each of them and he wondered if he was the only one who still thought they might live through this.

"I'm not leaving him," Mary May said.

Will turned sharply. He had little to say to this that he hadn't already said. Family made people do strange things, and though he thought in that instant she couldn't be more wrong, he also understood. Will would have fought through hell and back if he thought he could save his wife or daughter and preserve what little he had left.

"Okay," Will said. He didn't argue. He just went across the room as fast as he could, picked up the flak jacket and shotgun and shoved them toward Jerome and told the pastor they needed to hustle the fuck on.

Jerome looked wildly at Will but soon he had set the knife down and taken up the flak jacket in one hand and held the shotgun in the other. He looked back at Mary May now. "You should take this," he said to her, holding up the flak jacket.

"No," she said. "You should. If they mean to kill me they'll do it. No vest is going to stop that."

Will waited a half second, even though there was not a half second to give in this world and each passing moment brought them a little closer to whatever it was that was coming. He looked at Mary May. "Use the zip ties on the table there for his hands and then cut him loose from the chair. Get him outside and in front of John.

Don't let them inside here. You want to be in the open where more eyes are on you. John could have killed you at Eden's Gate but he didn't, that might still count for something now."

That was all the time he had for a good-bye and he went out the back door now with Jerome following. They came out into the night and the rough gravel there and looked about them, somewhat in wonder that they were still alone and no member of Eden's Gate stood waiting for them.

Grass grew in clumps here and there, but it was patchy at best with the shade of the house on one side and the rock cliff another twenty feet away leaving much of the land in shadow. The property itself was sloped and ran toward the road below. Will knew this. He knew every inch of this land and though it had been years since he had walked it, he still knew which way to go.

He crossed over the barren earth quickly and came to the face of the cliff just as fast. Jerome came shortly after, still carrying the flak jacket in one hand and the shotgun in the other. When he reached Will he glanced back at the house and the red sky farther on that was not daylight or dawn, but the burning of his own car in the darkness of the night. "We shouldn't have left her there alone," Jerome said.

Will kept running his hands up and over the rock face, he was looking it over, trying to retrace a path he'd taken years and years before. "I'm not leaving her," Will said now, finding the first handhold on the rock. "I'm climbing to the top of this thing. If she gets Drew outside I should have a shot on any who try to hurt her."

Jerome looked up at the cliff.

"My daughter discovered this when she was just eight years old," Will said. "There's hand and footholds for the first ten feet, and then we can sort of scramble our way to the top from there."

"You won't let anything happen to Mary May?" Jerome asked.

"If it comes down to it I'll use every bullet I have." He turned and looked Jerome over. The man had been at war but he looked now more like a civilian than anything Will remembered from his own time. "Give me the shotgun and put that vest on."

Jerome handed the shotgun over and Will strapped it down on the side of his pack then started up the rock face, using the hand and footholds he knew were there. Jerome tightened the vest down across his chest and soon was following.

"YOU DON'T HAVE TO DO THIS," DREW SAID.

He sat in the chair and one at a time she brought his hands forward on his lap, while his arms and chest were still secured beneath the rope. She zip-tied Drew's hands together at the wrists then sawed the knife back and forth across the ropes until they came loose. He stood now and she took the .38 from her waist, held it on him, and said, "I'm trying to save your life. Can't you see that?"

Drew smiled at her. "And I'm trying to save yours," he said.

She didn't know what to say to that. She thought of the young herder in the mountains. She thought about what he had said to her, "I hope you mean the same to him as he means to you." She did not know if that was true anymore. But she still wanted it to be.

She motioned toward the living room and the door there and he began to walk. She set the knife down as she passed the little table they had used for cooking. She followed him now with their father's .38 pointed directly at Drew's back. He put his bound hands on the doorknob then turned back to her, waiting on her go. "We leave this place and there's no going back," he said.

"There was no going back a long time ago," she said. "We passed that when Daddy died trying to get you off the mountain." She parted the blanket from the frame and looked out. John was waiting there. They had come nearly all the way up the hill now and they stood fifty feet away, twenty of them, if not more. All of them waiting on her as if they knew already she would come.

She went to Drew and placed the gun to his back and told him to turn the doorknob slow and let them out. They came out of the house linked this way, Drew out front and Mary May behind, holding the gun on Drew and walking after him.

Immediately she felt outside her element, sweat began to stand atop her skin and the feeling now was one of complete and utter terror. The line of people, women and men, constricting now upon her, all with weapons and all moving inward to encircle her as she went.

Mary May kept looking around at all the faces, half were people she knew—or thought she knew. One of her elementary school teachers was there. A couple farm workers she recognized from the bar that had not been in for years. A rancher her father had run cows for once upon a time. Many she knew by name and many more she knew by sight. These were people she might have said hello to on an afternoon, passing down the road like anyone else. She could hardly believe it. Drew had been right, Eden's Gate was everywhere. It was a virus, attacking any that came in contact with it and like any newly discovered virus it was slowly taking over before the cure could be found. She looked ahead of her now to where John stood, waiting on her and Drew.

"What's your plan here?" John called to her. He had done nothing but stand there and watch the two of them move toward him as Mary May pushed at Drew. Her nerves laced so tight within her that they might snap just from simply breathing.

"We're walking out of here," she said, still moving, but feeling at each step that the faces around her were closing in. She stopped now, seeing no opening in the crowd. She had thought in some way she'd be able to make one, that she'd wave the .38 around and they would part and she and Drew would just walk through. Now she stopped and she felt each and every one of them around her. She spun, holding the gun in her hand, keeping it low, but her eyes reaching out to each. "You know me," she said. "Some of you knew my parents. My family. You have to see this isn't right."

None of them said a thing to her and she spun again, the gun held a little higher. The faces that surrounded her were unchanged, cold as stone and just as unforgiving.

"Careful now," John said. "We're not the killers you think we are. We're farmers, we're shop owners, loggers, mill workers, delivery drivers, mothers, fathers, brothers, and sisters. We're like you. All of us. We're not killers like you think, so don't go waving that gun around. You might make someone jump who would rather not. Then where would we be?"

She held to her brother's shoulder now and kept the gun half raised. "How did you find us?" she asked.

"Finding you would imply we lost you to begin with," John said. He gave a wide look at the crowd around her. She was cut off now from the house and she could see each of them carried a weapon, from baseball bats to machetes to shotguns and assault rifles, they were armed not like any farmer or logger or anything else Mary May had ever seen. "Our people are always watching," John continued. "They're from every walk of life imaginable. Our faith is what unites us and our loyalty to one another is absolute. If someone attacks us, we attack back."

Mary May spun again, she couldn't trust them and there was ever the feeling of a spider crawling up her back. "I never attacked you," she said. "I was attacked."

"You were shown the way to Eden's Gate. You were shown the

same hospitality that all who come to Eden's Gate are shown. You think you are different but you are not." John looked around now, he looked to each face as if he were searching for a specific one from the crowd. "Where's Will?" he asked now. "I assume he is out there somewhere waiting, probably putting the crosshairs of that rifle scope on me as I speak." John looked now to the house, then he turned and looked to a far growth of pine at the edge of the property, his eyes still searching.

"You would think that we came for you, wouldn't you? But you've already been marked, Mary May. You've already been given the blessing of ink upon your chest. All that's left is for you to accept it." When John brought his eyes back to her, he said, "We did not come for you, Mary May. We came for Will. He has broken the bond of faith. He has turned his back on us. On his brothers and his sisters and The Father. We're not here for you, Mary May, we're here for him." John now motioned to two groups, three people in each, and they cut away. Mary May saw one group go into the house, while the other moved out across the property, keeping to the grasslands and slope below.

"Loyalty is important to us," John said. "I think I made that clear. We live our lives by specific rules, we listen only, and we learn and take our faith in The Father seriously, and any among us that would go against that faith and The Father's teachings, will find we do not forget and we do not forgive."

WILL JACKED THE BOLT FORWARD ON THE RIFLE AND ADVANCED the fresh cartridge. He lay atop the rock with a view down over the roof of the house to the group below. He had wondered about the walls of tattooed skins he'd seen and now he knew. Many he recognized but many more he did not know. They were from every-where, from this county and from places far beyond. Eden's Gate itself was everywhere, like a disease within the system that waits in silence, dormant until asked to attack every conduit of life, sucking blood from the vein and oxygen from the lungs.

Still winded from the climb, Will had moved up the rock face with the bag on his shoulders while Jerome followed, both men try-ing to move as fast and silently as possible. Both knowing that any missed step would send them falling over the edge, and any loos-ened rock would bring the attention of those below, and then in that moment they might wish they had fallen to begin with.

Now Will lay atop the rock trying to still his breath as he looked down at those below through the scope. He could see Mary May down there. He could see Drew before her and about ten feet far-ther on he saw John. At this distance, it was an easy shot and though Will could not tell what they were talking about, he kept his fin-ger on the trigger, the safety already pushed forward, ready at any hint of danger to take a shot. The chaos this might cause was the only way Will could see now that Mary May might escape. But he hesitated. He could not just pull the trigger. He had done it before but he had done it out of fear and in self-defense. This would be simply killing and he did not want to be that man. He was not that cold-blooded and he didn't want to be. He ran the scope around the circle of people and watched their every move, and he saw in them his own face and his own former desires.

A group of three was sent into the house and then another three were sent out and away from the larger group. Will moved the scope and followed this second group as they ran perpendicular to the house then into the larger darkness. The fire was still burning down at the base of the property and strange shadows were cast here and there that moved one way or another depending on the height and width of flame.

Will watched this group move and then, when he lost them among the far trees, he was quick to run the scope back to John and Mary May. Will called over his shoulder to Jerome, "Those three that went into the trees will likely come out and around on us in the next few minutes. Be ready with the shotgun. If they find us we might have to run. I'd rather that than get into a gun fight here atop the cliff."

MARY MAY HELD THE GUN STILL. SHE HAD ONE HAND ON HER brother's shoulder but she was looking around at John, feeling exposed. "You say you're not killers," Mary May said. "But my father went up the mountain and he never came back down. He died up there trying to get Drew and now I'm trying to do the same. That's what Daddy wanted and that's what I made my mind up to do."

"How?" John asked. "You've put your brother in front of you like he's your hostage. You've tied his hands like he's a prisoner. Why would you do that to your kin? Ask yourself that? Ask yourself why none among you, Will or Jerome, would allow this man to go free."

She looked around the group now, they were waiting on her, but none seemed to have raised their guns or weapons and she turned again and brought her eyes to John. "He's one of you. The Father or someone got in his head. He's not the same man he was. He's not the brother I knew when we were kids."

"No," John said. "He's better than that. His mind is open. His eyes are open. He has been changed. You are right in that."

"You talk as if it's a good thing that he turned his back on family."

John laughed. He looked around at the faces that looked back at all of them, the witnesses to whatever meeting this had become. "You still don't get it, do you? It was never about Eden's Gate. It was never a church issue. All The Father does is listen. He supports. That's something your own father never did. Your own father, and even your own community, turned their backs on Drew a long time before. The Father came to this place and saw what it could be. We had nothing to do with what passed between your own father and his children. That was not a church issue. That was a family one."

"But you killed him."

"We welcomed Gary. We knew about his wife, your mother. Our hearts went out to him. But we," John stopped now and raised his arms to encompass all of them. "We did not kill him. The Father did not kill him. I did not kill him. What your father wanted from Drew was not something we had any say in. Only Drew could answer to your father and his answer was no."

She felt her hand loosen from her brother's shoulder. She had known in some way. But it was beyond knowing, it was like an accident seen in the clear bright sunshine of day, but its action was so horrendous that in memory that same moment was as dark as night. Unseen, unwanted, and pushed away.

Drew turned all the way around now, his eyes seemed to her as cold as she had ever seen them. Hardened like two pieces of glass there within the sockets of his skull, unfeeling.

"Daddy made you proud," Drew said. "He gave you everything like it was your birthright and not mine to share. When we were kids, when we were teens, when we became adults together, he gave to you before he even thought to give to me. He gave you the bar, him and Mamma. And though there was a place there for me it was never mine to have."

She shook her head. She could not believe what she was hearing, or that their recollections of their life together could be so different in time and place. "No," she said. "I was just older."

"Older. Smarter. Funnier. Stronger. Nothing I did could ever measure up. All I tried to do in high school, all I did afterwards. It never was enough."

"No," she said. "That's not true."

"The truth," Drew said, "is that they never listened to me. They never tried to understand me. They never wanted me. Do you know what that's like? To live in a household and a family that doesn't want you?" He laughed now, the laugh carrying on into the silence. "Of course you don't."

"They loved you," she said. It was the only thing she could think to say. It was the truth and he needed to hear it. She could barely look at him. The hate she saw, the way he had grown taller almost as if talking about the death of their father had given him new life, while taking it from her, causing her to shrink ever farther now within herself. "Daddy loved you," Mary May said again, wanting him desperately to hear it.

"No. John is right. Daddy never listened to me. He never understood me. But The Father did. Eden's Gate did. They gave me a new life when they marked me, and baptized me, and then gave me the birth I always should have had, into the family I should have had." He turned now and looked at all the members of Eden's Gate who encircled them, and then he brought his eyes back to her. "I was given a new life and when Daddy came to get me I wanted nothing of the old life and I told him that. But it was like nothing had changed. It was the same between us. He did not listen. He insisted that his way was the true way and that I was in the wrong. He put his hands on me, but I was not the little boy he thought me to be. I had grown. My mind had grown. And whatever power he once had over me was gone."

"But it was a car accident," she said in a weak voice, not knowing what to say, not wanting to hear what he was telling her.

Drew looked at her like she was nothing. He looked at her like she was stupid. "You know that's not true," Drew said. "You've said that yourself. You just can't see it. You just can't picture how it was between us." Drew raised his two hands, banded together by zip ties at the wrist. His palms open and his fingers outstretched but tightening. "Picture him coming to me and trying to tear me out of the life I'd made. Picture his hands on me, trying to drag me away. And then picture the fact that I was finally stronger, faster, and quicker than he had ever been. Picture that and then you'll understand it was not an accident. That he forced my hand and he paid for all the wrong he'd done to me." He leaned in now, coming closer. "It was nothing to kill him. It was like sticking a knife into something already dead."

She fired from the waist and the bullet entered beneath her brother's chin and exited just behind his hairline. She watched his body go loose then fall all at once to the side. She felt like she was not there anymore. The night did not exist. The people. The pressure that had built within her with every one of his words. It all went out of her. It all ceased to exist for that one second as she watched him fall away.

Mary May was sobbing now, she had dropped the gun and she found herself upon the ground, trying to drag his body up to hers. The feel of his weight, the knowledge of what she'd done, of what she had allowed herself to do. She tried to tell herself that he had done this. But she knew he hadn't. She knew it was her that had pulled the trigger, that it was her and no one else.

She looked around now, they were all staring at her and as she raised her eyes to them they seemed to shrink back from her, to recede in some way. Soon, Mary May heard the shuffling of their movements. She held her brother in her arms. She tried to support his head, to hold him up. But she could do little for him now, she had shot him, hadn't she? But it did not feel like that. It did not feel as if it was her. It was slowly changing now. The anger she had felt, the rage, the sheer compulsion of her action that seemed to have come from her like lightning from a storm, natural as anything she had ever felt.

"Your father made you proud," John said. John stood in the same place he had stood before, but his people were filing past now, moving one at a time away from him and down the slope again. "I gave you the sin of envy, but I see now that you were neither the pride your father gave you nor the envy I saw in you. Now I see that I should have given you wrath. Someday when the time is right for you to accept that, I will be waiting for you."

She looked at him. He was a blur within the lineaments of her vision, tears now streaming down her face. "You didn't come for Will," she said. "You came to tell me about Drew. You came to see what I would do. It was not me that pulled the trigger. It was you." She was fighting back tears now. Her vision was almost gone in the aftermath of it all.

"Drew went against us when he killed your father. And we could not forget or forgive him for his sin, for he had told us his envy was gone and we, foolishly had believed he followed in the true path The Father had set for him."

She blinked. She tried to understand what was happening. Somehow her brother was dead. Somehow he was laying in her arms, and John stood over them now, telling her it was her brother who had done this to himself, telling her he deserved all that he had received. "You did this to him," she said again. "It was you and not some other. It was you and The Father that killed him."

John stood there. He looked her over as if she were his own

creation come to life. "Your father made you proud. He made you think you could not be touched, that you were right in all you did. But you were not. We came as witnesses," John said, now moving his arms to show her he meant all the members of Eden's Gate who had come with him and now were moving past him down the hill. "We came to witness what you did to your brother—what your family did to him. We did not do this. You did. And we will hold this over you for all time. We will control you in this way. It is important you understand this, Mary May. You were never right and now you have become the sin I did not see in you. You have become wrath, and I will always remember you and be ready to help you, for I too was wrong. I was wrong about you, Mary May. You are wrath and I will be the one to take that sin from you one day."

WILL COULD NOT BELIEVE IT. THE WORLD THROUGH THE SCOPE always acted in silent pantomime. The characters at such a distance as to be rendered mute, only seen in movements that mirrored those of the real world, but that were somehow not of the real world. The sound of the bullet had made it real.

It had cut through the distance as if through glass dividing one place from another. He watched Drew fall. He watched Mary May move to him, and now, as he watched through the scope, Will saw John standing there, speaking to her in silence once again.

He pulled his eye back from the rifle scope. He had to blink and to wipe the sweat away. Through it all his eyes were on Mary May below and John standing over her. Every member of Eden's Gate now moved back down the hill, as if Drew's death had been the point all along. As if this somehow was what they had come for, all of them filing past John after bearing witness to this act.

"Was it her?" Jerome asked now. He stood above Will, and with the shotgun and the vest he looked every part God's sentinel here on earth.

"I think so," Will said. "I think she shot him. I think she shot Drew and I feel I know why."

"What does this mean now?" Jerome asked. "What does this mean for Mary May or for Eden's Gate?"

Will wiped a finger beneath his eye again. He felt the damp moisture of his sweat. His mind was going a hundred different places, but as he put his eye to the scope again, he watched John there and then after some final word, John was gone, following as the last of his people filed past. The back of John's head now indistinguishable from all the rest, as if they were him and he was them. "It means they have a secret they can hold over her and though she will try to fight it, there is nothing you or I, or even Mary May can do about it. The sooner we all realize that the better."

"I don't accept that," Jerome said. "No one is beyond help. Not you or me or Mary May."

Will said nothing. It was a mess. It was all a fucking mess and there was no way he could see his way out of it. But he knew they would try.

V

No one believes death is coming until the moment it does. And most still refuse to believe it even then.

—THE FATHER, EDEN'S GATE
Hope County, Montana

WILL HAD ABOUT THE SAME FEELING HE'D HAD WHEN HE came back from the war, like nothing had been accomplished, but he thought now maybe the accomplishment wasn't about winning a war, it was about surviving. It was about coming back alive from a place so few were able to come back from. That was the accomplishment and it's what drove him now as he skirted the tree line with the broad Junegrass field before him and the place he had thought of as home for the past twelve years, the cabin Eden's Gate had given him up there on the hill.

Holly and three men from Eden's Gate were waiting up there at his place. And as far as Will could tell they'd been waiting for several days now. From out of the shadows he watched them. He watched them up there as they brought furniture out and burned it in the night, bits of wood, the mattress he had slept on, clothes, the single chair and table he had within. Holly often came to the edge of the hill where he had once stood to watch the bear. The woman watching not for bear as Will had done, but watching for Will as if he now were the threat that bear had been — something dangerous out there in the greater wilderness, something lost, something looking for its next kill.

But Will was none of that now. He was a survivor. He had made it back but he could see now that this was not his home, not at least in the way it once had been. Nothing in Hope County was the way it once had been.

But Will took his time, careful now. He watched them through the night then into the day. He waited in the woods as the men went to piss, close enough then to hear the urine hit the ground and to hear the breathing of each man as they relieved themselves. He watched them go for water then return, using the same buckets Will himself had used for so many years. He watched them eat his food and plunder the stores he had set aside and he watched them make themselves at home in the home that had once been his.

When he left, a day later, nothing had changed for him in all his studying of the place. It was not his home anymore and he knew it had stopped being that a while back. He followed the river for a quarter of the day and he often stopped to glass the land beyond. He did not know what he was searching for but he knew wherever he went he would be okay. He could live off the land if he needed to. He could go back to the old ways. He could use the knowledge that had been handed down to him through the generations. He had snares and traps. He had cartridges and the rifle, he had clothes, and anything he did not have he could make or forage.

His plan was to dig in deep. Get back into the woods and into the mountain valleys and rocky strongholds of the range and make a place among the trees and crags. He thought now about all that had been attempted. He'd paid a price for what he'd done. Perhaps Eden's Gate and The Father had been right about him all along, about his sin. About the demon that lived inside of him, that would not let him forget the sins he'd inflicted on his enemies and on all he loved. Will had thought somehow that helping Mary May would give him solace. He wondered now if it had.

He thought about all there was yet to do. He did not have an answer for any of the thoughts roaming about his mind yet, and he crossed upriver, using the shallows to skirt back and forth along the waterway, moving ever farther north. The rocky outcroppings grew around him as he went and the feeling that things unseen were closing in on him, moving in the shadows and thickets he crossed through or following along beside him on the high spines of rock that often cut the light from the river valley down below.

He felt haunted by this feeling and often he paused midstride, or even halfway across a series of stones that spanned the river, and he would turn his eyes back on the path he'd taken and his ears would try to pick the slightest irregularity from the rush of water and overhead breeze. He thought about Eden's Gate. He thought about those men who had been waiting for him at his cabin. He thought about the ghosts that followed him and what they wanted.

In a sense Will had saved Mary May, but it was not the kind of salvation any of them had wished for, or even thought to expect. He had come down off the cliff with Jerome and they had seen her there holding her brother and Will had wondered whether that brother in death was different than the brother in life and whether those two could ever be the same, as Mary May had so desperately wanted him to be.

Will knew that feeling, too. He knew what followed him through the trees and up the river was not anything he could touch or hold. It was an idea of the loved ones he had left behind, it was guilt and hope, it was memories of a past life that he thought might not be his life at all. He knew that feeling just as Mary May did now. He knew how one remakes the past in the image they want to see of the future. He could not blame her for that, people had been doing the same for millennia and it was nothing new to have hope, to want to try and make a change. It was nothing new to deny the past and embrace the future.

He set his bag down when he came to a little glade that ran a quarter mile up the valley, lined on all sides by paper birch and the thick underbrush of the mountain. He crossed to the river with his canteen and dipped it and watched the bubbles rise in the slow current, and then he drank fully. The water overflowed at the edges of his mouth and ran down through the scraggly hair of his beard. He realized now that he was half wild, that he had most likely been half wild even when all this had started and Lonny had come to him asking about the bear.

There were stores he had taken from the house he had shared with his wife and daughter, and he took a can of green beans out now and pried the top off with the opener he had taken from there as well. He had let himself into the house for only a moment and filled the bag with what he could, then left without a last good-bye to the house or the memories there. He knew they were never truly gone to begin with. He hoped that was something Mary May might learn about herself as well.

The sun was out above and he sat with his back leaning against the pack, his hat tipped down to shade his eyes. He dipped a finger down into the beans and then pulled them out one at a time. He ate them that way, keeping his eyes always on the shadows beneath the trees and the path the water cut among the rocks that lined it and the greater forest all around. There was something out there that was not memory or ghost and it was watching him from out of the forest he had passed through only minutes before.

Without moving but to set the can down and to gather up the rifle, Will watched the place among the brush that he was sure held whatever presence hunted him. He watched the shift of the brush, the way it caught and pulled, like something back there had taken hold. He stood now and moved closer, his feet cautious as they went. Will ready to run if he needed to, or ready to shoot, or simply ready for whatever it might be.

The flash of brown was the first thing he saw. The bush moved again and he saw the fur. It was a grizzly bear, but he could not tell its height or girth or anything more than that he was not alone. He thought of the big boar grizzly he had seen in the lightning storm that night. He thought of that same bear seen across the river a couple days later, probably returned to whatever haunts it had before. But Will knew it had not disappeared, that nothing disappeared, wherever it went it was always somewhere, like a ghost or like a memory that never seemed to fade.

The brush moved again. He could hear breathing. He could hear great lungs working and the movement of air. A branch snapped somewhere beyond and he almost jumped, pivoting slightly with the rifle still held in his hand. He did not know what was out there. Will had killed many in his life. Those that walked upright on two legs and those that walked on all four, and he had known even then that a price was owed. He was a sinner. He had taken and taken, and though he had tried to give back, he felt always that it was not enough.

He thought of his family back there in the cemetery in Fall's End, he thought of Mary May and Jerome and all of Hope County. He knew all that had come to pass was only the beginning. He knew that whatever waited for him out there in the darkness, whether it was a grizzly bear or something else, was waiting for him still and would be waiting for as long as he chose to look away.

He took one step then another. He put a hand out to the brush and pulled away a branch. There was darkness beyond. An unknowable void that asked now for him to enter and see what had followed him for hours, and for days, and possibly for all the years of his life.

THERE WAS A GRAVE FOR DREW DOWN IN THE CHURCHYARD NOW. In the days that passed Mary May would go there and she would stand over the three of them and see the varying shades of green atop each one. Her mother's grave was the oldest, then her father's, and then Drew's. The same dirt color as had been the earth through which Mary May and Jerome had dug themselves. Working in the nighttime to get the hole dug out six feet deep. Everyone in the town knowing what they were doing and none stopping to say a thing, none pausing, or even surprised to see another hole go in the ground and a body soon to follow.

The sheriff was the only one to stop by and really spend any time looking down into the pit they'd dug. He stood there, pushed up his hat with a finger, and looked down into that hole. When he finally brought his eyes to Mary May, he said, "I guess this means you found your brother."

"Yes, it does." Mary May sat in the shade next to Jerome. They had been working all through the night and into the morning and the sun had not yet fully crested above the church roof, leaving half the cemetery still in shadow.

"What did he die of?"

"His heart gave out."

"That right?" the sheriff asked.

"That's right."

"Where are you keeping the body?" the sheriff asked.

"The county coroner's office, same as where they took Mamma and Daddy."

She could see him studying her. He turned and looked to the two other graves then turned and looked back at her. "If I go in there and ask what happened to him are they going to tell me his heart gave out?"

"I don't know why they wouldn't," she said. "The coroner seemed to give it to us straight when Daddy was in there. An accident, I believe."

"That's what they called it at the time."

"Did they change their minds?"

"No, not that I know of. But it's getting hard to look past the circumstances here before us."

"What circumstances are those?"

"Three dead from the same family in nearly the same amount of weeks. That's something that is a little hard to overlook."

Mary May looked up at him. "You said it, Sheriff."

"I know I did." He was shaking his head and looking down at the grave again. "You think if I go in there and ask that coroner what happened he will give it to me straight?"

"Is the coroner still bearded?" Mary May asked.

"Last I checked."

"Sure," Mary May said. "I bet he gives it to you just as straight as he did when Daddy died."

The sheriff turned and looked to where Jerome sat on the meager grass beside Mary May. He had taken his collar off. He sat sweating with the first few buttons of his shirt undone and his sleeves rolled up over his elbows. "What do you say about all this?" the sheriff asked.

"Faith is a powerful thing," Jerome said.

SHE CLEANED A GLASS THEN SET IT DOWN ON THE BACK BAR AND reached and brought up another. She was at this work five minutes before the double cab went by with four men inside, the truck pulling a horse trailer behind. The brakes were heard next and the muted tinge of the brake lights seen in the frames of the barroom windows.

There was a baseball bat she kept on a shelf below her, and she reached and stood it beside her with the handle leaning on the bar. The brake lights went out now and there was the sound of a door opening then the clap of it closing once again. She continued to clean the glasses and watched the thin figure move past in the shaded tint of the glass then come to the door and push it open.

"Hey there," she said.

"You open?" the young sheepherder asked. She could see he was bruised badly about one cheek, but the bruise was fading and it didn't stop him from smiling at her when he spoke.

"In thirty minutes."

The young herder stood looking around at the place, then he stepped up and took a stool as if he had been in her bar a thousand times before. "I guess you found your brother," he said.

"I found him."

"And he was the same as you remembered?"

"He was my brother but he was not the same."

"I hate to hear that." He looked around the bar now, at the chairs that sat atop the tables, and then he looked back at her. "Let me help you," he said.

"Help me?"

"Yeah, I can take down the chairs. How old were you when you started working here?"

"How old are you?"

"Fifteen."

"I wasn't much older than you. My parents used to own this place." She watched him move away and take one chair down after another.

"So it's in the blood?" he asked.

"Yes."

"And you won't leave it?"

"No," she said. She was watching him now. He had taken the third chair down off the table and she told him to sit in it. She poured him a water and set it down on the table before him. "I grew up here, right in this bar." She smiled at him now. "I had my first kiss out back with some dumb cowboy. I wasn't much older than you then. Almost got caught by my dad. Fuck, he loved this place. He loved it so much he couldn't see that it was staying the same and the world around it was changing. I see that now. I see that clearer than he ever did."

"Then they haven't scared you off yet?" the boy asked.

"No," she said. "They haven't scared me. They took my mom, my brother. Daddy did what he could but it wasn't enough."

"You're the only one left now, aren't you?"

"I'm not the only one," she said. "There are others like me who see the world changing and want to do something about it."

"And you're going to do that here?"

"No better place," she said.

She watched him look her over. He stood now from the chair and she knew he would leave. "I'll tell them about this place when we get there. I'll tell them about you."

"Where is there?"

"*There* is wherever this place isn't," the boy said. "It doesn't matter to us. My father is driving me and a couple others out of here. I'll find someone that cares and I'll tell them about this place."

"And you think that will make a difference?"

The boy shook his head. "I don't know. All the things we've seen up there on that mountain, it certainly made a difference with me." He looked away, out to where the truck was waiting for him. "That's what you're doing back here," he said. "Trying? I guess all of us have to try in some way, don't we?"

"Yes," she said. "We do."

ACKNOWLEDGMENTS

This novel wouldn't exist without the fans who have made all the Far Cry games such a success. Thank you for your faith in these worlds, and these stories, and the characters that lend them humanity.

For me video games have always been an escape from the real world, but as video games began to reach new heights, that escape seemed to matter less and less, and the real world and the world of the video game began to merge. In this way video games became something else, not an escape, but something even more powerful and valuable to me. Something that required not just the willingness of the player to be involved and engaged within these worlds, but also the knowledge and understanding of what it is to be human, to see that human condition from many different perspectives and to sympathize with and understand them all. In short, the world of the video game has in many ways become like that of another world I have long found my own salvation within—the world of the novel.

I want to thank Ubisoft for creating some of the best video games this world has ever seen, and for pushing that world ever further with each new iteration and release. I want to thank my team at Ubisoft, Caroline Lamache, Anthony Marcantonio, and Victoria Linel, for reading my past novels and bringing this opportunity to me. This has long been a dream of mine. Thank you for bringing it ever closer with each new draft.

For the people of Ubisoft Montreal who are innovators and

leaders in this industry, I want to give a specific thank you to Dan Hay, David Bédard, Jean-Sébastien Décant, Nelly Kong, Manuel Fleurant, and Andrew Holmes for answering my many questions and bringing me behind the curtain. I am continually impressed by just how much work and effort goes into building not just the game of Far Cry, but the universe that surrounds it from the ground up.

I like to think I'm older and wiser now that I've made a living at this for the past eight years, but the truth is I'm still learning. And though this is my fourth novel, each time it is different, and each path to publication takes new turns and new directions and I would not have made it if it was not for the people who supported me and who gave me the space to write this novel.

Nat, you've been there through all of this. Even from the first story you read of mine in a small literary journal. Thanks for always giving me your best.

To the Mineral School Artist Residency and to the founder, Jane Hodges, thank you for the classroom space where much of this novel was written. To Debra DiDomenico, who is a constant in every acknowledgment I have written, thank you for your support and for introducing me to the Darrington boys and the property there. Tom Heye, your cabin was instrumental in the first iterations of this novel. Jim Haney, Rick Knight, and David Gronbeck, thank you for making the property in Darrington the beautiful place it is today and for opening that place up to me and making me feel welcome there. Thank you.

To Mary Perkins and Ernie Seevers, you two gave me a wonderful studio where I could disappear day after day, and amid all the chaos of everyday life that place became my constant. Thank you.

And speaking of everyday chaos, I would have none of this if it wasn't for my wife, Karen, who somehow puts up with all my mental and physical absence while writing. You have always been there for me and there isn't a thank you I can say or give that will ever be big enough, but I'll keep trying. To you, and to my parents and yours, thank you for helping to raise our children. TiTi and Poppy, Gong Gong and Poh Poh, you guys make this all possible and, most important of all, you kept us all sane. Thank you.

ABOUT THE AUTHOR

Urban Waite is a good guy who writes evil things. His debut novel, *The Terror of Living*, was named a Best Book of the Year by *Esquire*, *The Boston Globe*, and *Booklist*. His second novel, *The Carrion Birds*, was a finalist for the New Mexico and Arizona Book Award, and called "a candidate for best crime book of 2013" by the *New York Journal of Books*. His third novel, *Sometimes the Wolf*, was *The Sun Sentinel*'s pick for Best Book of the Year. His short fiction has appeared in the *Best of the West* anthology, the *Southern Review*, and many other journals. His work has been translated into nine languages and is available in more than twenty countries worldwide.